Malingering

malingering

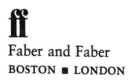

**Stories
by
Susan Compo**

ff
Faber and Faber
BOSTON ■ LONDON

Copyright © 1993 by Susan Compo

Library of Congress Cataloging-in-Publication Data

Compo, Susan.
    Malingering : short stories / by Susan Compo.
       p.   cm.
    ISBN 0-571-19818-X
    1. City and town life—California—Los Angeles—Fiction.
2. City and town life—England—London—Fiction. 3. Los
Angeles (Calif.)—Fiction. 4. London (England)—Fiction.
I. Title.
PS3553.04839M35   1993
813'.54—dc20   93-10886
                                                          CIP

This is a work of fiction. All characters and events are products of the author's imagination. The author's use of names of actual persons, living or dead, is incidental to the purposes of the plot and is not intended to change the fictional nature of this work.

Cover design by Lorna Stovall

Printed in the United States of America

Contents

Preface

i wrote this collection almost entirely to the strains of so-called "Music of Your Life" stations that play songs from bygone days lived by those presumably now in their golden years. Many of the songs had out-of-tempo, almost prosaic introductions, so in contrast to their picnic–happy refrains.

Malingering comes in as gothic-rock or death-rock broodingly edges and slumps toward its inherent extinction. One character, Sharlott, dismisses the affected-gloom-look as suiting "only the very young . . . redundant for everyone else, the way style became fate."

Time skips in a kind of unnatural surrealism — I'm too far north for any other kind. The world in these pages means London, Los Angeles, Orange County, and Fargo, North Dakota, interwoven with various other extremes, as in theme parks. Characters, among them gossip columnists, plagiarizing poets, jaded romance writers, and deconstructionist comedians, are usually on a distracted search, looking for the living and dead, the famous (if only to the seekers). American gothic psychos rub shoulders and more with North London ravers. Cats usually point the way out with their articulated tails; but then, who's counting?

Introductions

He Pales Next to You

Doubts about creating and experiencing art besiege a jaded romance writer, who is mistaken for a sleuth-scribe by an even further deluded young man.

Ad Astra per Aspera

Holly's home has a rotted wood floor with unusual patchwork. Surfer Jay, a sometime-jewelry designer, learns just how close to suffering he'll go for inspiration.

The Jealousy Loan

Simonetta searches for her mother, whom she is certain is the same age as she. What she encounters is as odd as her origins. Refracted new romantics, punk ghosts, and a small, insistent pooch co-exist in London and Los Angeles . . . and some never-never places in between.

Who Is Sleepwalking (And Who Envies Them)?

Sleepwalking, suggested slang for sex, places a pizza-delivery boy in a pond scum–shaded haunted house, and an Orange County theme-park teen in the arms of her boyfriend's look-alike.

A Stay-in Story

A welcome wake-up call, for one who loathes to see the sun, comes late one night. Can angels help, or do their wings just get in the way? And are cats receptive or simply perceptive?

High on Hope

There's always one I can't find an excuse for.

Like Goth Never Happened

Suppose Olive had come up later and missed what were her formative, charmless-school years? If she'd never known Nell and only met Aidan, with his loose jeans and baggy tea, listening to his bright sounds devoid of any downbeat, it'd be—it'd be like goth never happened.

(Don't Quit) Your Day Job

A hapless gossip columnist stumbles into the tale that wags the tongues. If she only could keep her facts as straight as her hair . . .

Stiletto Life

Anthropomorphic schisms and mind over Mattel, spurred on by shoes that fit and start in escalator grates.

For N., Who Won't Want It

Of awards and other imaginary things: in Fargo, love is closer than Bonnie thinks. But does she care?

The Continuity Girl

Lorella's absent-minded point of view originates *from*, not *of*, the Hollywood sign. She wants to be a recluse, yet needs Outside for ideas. Soon, she's caught between two places: one faintly forgotten and the other, disarmingly unfamiliar.

Operation: Estrangement

Tamira has one burning ambition while Peepers is the time-shared cat who swallows Canary Wharf.

Hazy-ography

The best malingerer knows how to retain belief.

He Pales
Next to You

*i*n a railway cafe on Gypsy Hill, the tea white was like grist, or at best, two warring substances grafted together. Sharlott reluctantly drank it anyway—she'd have been happier on a steady diet of poison. Crumbs from the tabletop stuck to her wrists; the counter just behind was laminated with grease.

Sharlott had left her South London home that morning, made an effigy of pillows to exaggerate her body and stuck a note like a backstage pass to the one that stood for her chest. "Out of my life I've made a crawling disaster," she'd written. "Not by a miracle I'll endure."

A handful of men entered the cafe and Sharlott gazed at the swirls of mud on their rubber boots. Sharlott nodded and looked down at her half-eaten plate of chips. Her hair, to her elbows, was platinum and wavy, like the crinkled fries on her dish.

The man who had smiled was seated now and slowly sipping his own cup of tea. He kept staring at Sharlott, so she picked up her fork to pantomime eating. She shifted slightly away in her chair to avoid further responding to him—she felt about as sensual as a fossil as she swallowed a soggy, lukewarm french fry whole, as if it were a worm.

Sharlott turned her thoughts to the night before, when she'd dreamt she was sleeping in a cocoon made of thorns, surrounded by a panorama of foot-in-the-grave men. They silently watched her sleep, secretly waiting for her to turn and be periled. Sharlott awoke to find her boyfriend next to her, but across the bed and ensnared in the coverlet. She was left cold, exposed, sick of it; so, as if she were warding off an invasion of ghosts, she plotted her escape.

As she rose from the table, she knotted her paisley scarf under her chin and picked up her denim jacket. As a parting gesture, she brought the rough and nubbly napkin to her painted lips and kissed it with indifference.

In near-summer South London, Sharlott stood on a subway platform, with no idea where to go.

◻◼◻

Damien woke when a slice of sunlight hit his eyes like a white blindfold. The drapes were blackout quality, so the brightness was all the more disturbing. He looked over to ask Sharlott to fix them but in her place he saw the ridiculous shape, fat and dimpled as clotted cream.

The pledge-like note she'd left was so stupid, he hated what she'd written about her interior versus exterior life. Damien covered the paper with one of his own pillows, snuffed out the mock-urgency of the words. But he had to get out of bed to adjust the curtains and after he did, he was compelled to peek in Sharlott's wardrobe, to gauge the depth of her escape. A small, soft bag was missing, as was some of the more extreme Vivienne Westwood. She'd left the leather jacket he'd given her, that he'd hand-painted with the name and logo of his group: Likeness Kiss, it said, in elaborate pastel blocks on the back, now pressed up against her knee-length mohair sweater.

Damien yawned, knew that in this case, she couldn't stay away that long.

☐■■

On her headphones Sharlott listened to an early Siouxsie and the Banshees tape. She'd caught the first tube from Waterloo, a train pristine and interior-still, its dirt having settled in overnight. At Embankment. she changed for the verdant District Line, and aimed for Kew.

Some youths got on the car with her and sat opposite—they must have been out all night and then stranded by lack or infrequency of transport. One boy wore a distressed t-shirt bearing the face of one of

Sharlott's friends. Really it was a friend of Damien's, but Sharlott had gone out with the guy once anyway, on the sly. They'd gone to a football match and stood near the goalposts. It had been so cold the man, then a fledgling pop star, used Sharlott as the lining of his greatcoat. Afterward, outside an Indian restaurant in Shepherd's Bush, he'd kissed her, twisting into the small of her back the heel of a shoe she'd broken. Sharlott remembered he'd said he'd keep the fat black heel "as proof," and that he was either married or engaged at the time. Her hair was long and lavender then, that she was sure of.

She looked again at the face on the t-shirt, its full lips highlighted black. There was a tiny strand of pearls he'd bought her in Rye; they were hidden and chipped in a drawer of her smaller bureau.

The boy across from her stared back now, so Sharlott looked away.

Years ago Sharlott had been signed by an artist, had her paint-splattered shirt autographed while she was still wearing it. When she was promoting her first book (when she was still hungry), she'd eagerly repeated this story to the press. She'd underscored how from that moment on she'd decided to live as a painting would, not realizing then it could backfire in the most insipid ways: she might find herself covered in old coats, suddenly blanketless, defenseless in museums, gawked at.

" 'Scuse me," said the bearer of the t-shirt, "ain't I seen you on Breakfast TV?"

"No," replied Sharlott, and the boys exited quietly at the next stop.

When the train occasionally went above ground, it was still shrouded in darkness. The morning sky was too weighty to permit dawn, and Sharlott looked across into the tight black funnel, its suffocating curves before and behind. She stared through the glass, but however much she feigned looking at nothing, it was the reflected contours of her face she was assessing: the shadows of her cheeks, the overstated high bones. Her pale lips met like flat rowed fields.

If she went ahead to Kew, she realized, there was still a ways to go. She could read; some might write, but she never would, not in public anyway. Besides, she felt her work was overrated; she neglected to acknowledge its singular ability to make hers seem the only authentic experiences. Instead she thought it shallow as an ink-well of wishes—a vat in which she still treaded, knowing it was really only sink or drown.

Sharlott's boyfriend, Damien, had a tendency to frequent goth- or death-rock clubs, which she hated, considering the patrons to be the deceased who forgot to lie down. The affected gloom-look suited only the very young, she thought, and was redundant for everybody else, the way style became fate.

What Damien's fascination was for the now all-but-buried scene, Sharlott couldn't figure. As a sci-fi rockabilly star, it really wasn't his picture. She had asked him once, when they were outside the Kit-Kat Club near Charing Cross station. Damien laughed his reply and insisted that he liked the way the club-goers parted their hair.

Sharlott hadn't stayed in the Kit-Kat very long, and was an ochre-crowned swimmer struggling against the crowd, certain that the gathered wore yards of tulle, layers of lace, and accentuated features just to make it that much harder for her to move through them.

For no reason she could reach, it reminded her of going to a drive-in movie when she was a child in central California. One time in particular she'd seen a hearse there, parked large amongst the smaller, more intimidated cars that had flocked to see *Love Story*.

The train came to a complete halt and Sharlott found she'd missed her stop, Kew. She got out at Richmond station and walked in search of another cafe, tea becoming the primary focus of her aimlessness. But she just went around the taxi circle, ending up back inside the station, where she had a paper cup of tea and a dark chocolate bar.

Sharlott rented a locker for her suitcase and left Richmond station again to walk along the Twickenham side of the river. From a dock to her left a man accompanied by an odd-eyed dog called to Sharlott. "Going across?" She looked down to see three passengers—a woman with a small, especially animate child, and a tall youth—in a tiny boat, and she walked to join them.

She sat at the bow of the boat, about as far as she could get from the youth, who was actually about her age. She tried not to take in his shaggy hair (which was a rather magnetic shade of silver-magenta) or the uneasy expression on his striking face. There was only the sloshing sound of water as they drifted to the other side. Sharlott paid the boatman, patted the weary dog on the head, and followed the lead made by the hand-holding woman and child as they walked up the hill.

Her pace was not fast enough, and a shadow soon appeared over her left shoulder. "Pardon me," a voice said, "but don't I know you?"

"I don't think so," she replied. The young man, who'd now covered his lurid hair with a frilly scarf, persisted. "No, I'm certain I do."

"Really," Sharlott regretted.

"Yes," he said. "Name's Simon. Are you going to Ham House?"

"Are you?"

"Richmond Park. But if you're taking in Ham House, perhaps I will too. It's this way." He pointed to a gate followed by some rough-edge steps.

The house was several yards beyond and they toured the cold, H-shaped edifice, which was filled with marble floors and twisted columns. Tapestries did nothing to warm the place; in fact, their faded darkness made it all the more chilling. In the queen's bedchamber, Simon leaned over to Sharlott and whispered, "I like my bed better. I have a black net over it." Sharlott smiled with just her lips and spun away.

In the withdrawing room she stared at some wool

and velvet armchairs—their wavy fabric matched her long coat. She descended the great staircase and bumped into Simon on the middle landing.

"There you are!" he said. "Have you seen the garden?"

She walked the circumference of the seventeenth-century garden while Simon sat on a stone bench. Finally, she joined him there as if they were the two remaining players in a game of musical chairs.

"Why don't you come with me to Richmond Hill? I think there's a spot at the top where we can have refreshment."

"No, thank you, really."

"Please. I'd love your company."

By the time they'd scaled Richmond Hill, Sharlott was desperately out of breath. Her faux–fur-trimmed boots had sunk again and again in the soft ground that was more mud than grass. At the cafeteria-style restaurant, she had yet another tea to Simon's coffee. As she removed the golden foil from the oblong pad of butter, Simon gasped, a sound Sharlott knew well.

"I know who you are!" he said. "You're that writer. You do those mysteries."

Sharlott's work could hardly be classified as mysteries but she was relieved to let it go, preferring it to a correct assumption.

"This could be kismet," he said. "You could be just the person to help me. You see, the real reason I'm here is because of my girlfriend. Well, actually I was married at the time, but not to her — it's all rather complicated."

"I can tell."

"No, seriously. There was this girl. She was mad, but I loved her. I mean, once I'd lost her, I knew I'd loved her. And now I've heard from someone that she's had my child, even called it Simonetta, but try as I might I can't find them or her anywhere. Nowhere."

"Mmmm . . . "

"I did get a note from her once, all scribbled and loopy and saying I'd find her where four winds met, and something about low moss-covered walls, but until this morning I never took that to mean Richmond Hill. But when I woke up this morning I thought, 'That's it, Richmond Hill.' "

"All this in the sleeping net, of course."

"Yes! Well, under it, more like."

"Well, is she here?"

Simon looked around the dining room. "No, of course not. But there's a clearing over by the deer park — the ash pit, I think it's called, they used to bury plague victims there. That's where I'm going to look."

Sharlott knew it was irresponsible of her not to tell him she was no mystery writer, that her work was more like jaded romances, but she was hooked, intrigued. Too, he seemed so sincere that she thought her confession might visibly break his heart or embarrass him into inertia.

They walked through Richmond Park to the clearing, the ash heap. "Maybe we should separate,"

Sharlott suggested. She wandered off to the edge of the clearing where a pale man was sitting, the back of his head pressed against a tree trunk. He looked like a direct descendant of those who didn't survive the black death: his teeth were dark and he was so thin it was as if his bones were made up of the white noise that comprises heroin.

Simon surrendered, offered a theatrical shrug toward Sharlott, who was still some distance away. She felt sorry for him then and when near, she agreed to have dinner in his Battersea flat.

Once there, in the kitchen portion shadowed by the shell of Battersea power station, he handed her a glass of mineral water. "To the ghosts who part their hair," he proposed, and Sharlott started to say she felt it unlucky to toast with non-alcoholic beverages. But instead she inwardly tried to deny the similarity between Simon's and Damien's phrases.

Simon motioned to a table with one place setting, and Sharlott said she thought that a table set for one is a table begging for a seance.

He smiled. "Here," he said, thrusting photographs into her palms. "There are pictures of my girlfriend. She's called Honor. The photos are all I have left of her, what's she's been reduced to."

Sharlott studied one overexposed picture of a girl at a graveyard. "She kind of resembles what's-his-name from The Cure," she said, to make light of how sad she really felt at seeing Honor.

"True. She tried to."

"Has it occurred to you . . . it is possible that she could be dead?"

"No—no ghost. Haunter, maybe, but no ghost."

"Are you sure? I mean, ghosts aren't always overt in making themselves known. They very well might just do something shy, give a clue for you to catch on to. Our belief in them is naturally more crucial than their belief in us."

Simon shrugged, brought out a warmed quiche, which he placed in the center of the table. He carved a triangular piece for Sharlott.

"You know what I saw today when we were in Richmond Park?" Sharlott was drunk with tiredness, now that the food had taken away the sharp insistence of hunger. "This guy, I think he used to be in Siouxsie and the Banshees. He's probably been wandering there for ages, with no one any wiser."

"No one ever remembers me either," Simon replied.

"Maybe that's a tribute to your etherealness."

"Yeah, thanks." Her compliment had made him shy.

While Simon cleared the dishes, Sharlott surveyed his room. She envied him his organized decay, his cozy life of anonymous non-existence. She ended up staying in his flat, in her own corner of his bed, caressed only by the black netting. At midnight, just before she fell asleep, she felt the awkward rebirth of the hour, the shaky hint of something new.

Sharlott would have left at the first intimation of dawn, but she had nowhere to go. So she stayed to

face the unsure half-life that was midday, light filtered
through dusty bark-cloth drapes and embellished by
asterisk-shaped particles.

She whispered her story to Simon.

"It's like," she said of her relevance to Damien, "like
I'm forced to perform these dramatic shows of emotion, these extravagant gestures . . . but my heart's
not in it. And it's a wonder he can't see that, can't see
through me."

"It's okay," Simon replied. "You can stay here with
me as long as you like."

"But I can't. I can barely be in the same room with
anyone else, at any time."

"I know my flat is small," he said softly. "But I'm on
the dole, you see, and I'm lucky to have even this."

"I'm sorry, no—I didn't mean that. I didn't mean
your place. It's me. The whole situation's with me."
Sharlott paused, to draw breath. "Maybe I can find a
hotel nearby."

"Near is best," Simon answered, pulling her to him.

If there were a drug to keep people from love,
Sharlott would have, in that moment, walked down
midnight, imperiled, glass-stained alleys to score it, to
take it toward overdose.

Instead, resigned, she went with Simon to a nearby
pub. In the Tirra Lirra, they drank their plowman's
lunches and toasted—properly this time—their fates.

"Well," she shrugged, "it's like Damien always says,
'The best things are visited upon those who happen to

be looking the other way.' " Simon winced as their glasses clinked.

Sharlott found a bed-and-breakfast near Brompton Cemetery, next to a building site. For a few days she didn't call Simon but one night she did phone Damien, only to hang up at the first note of his expectant voice. Damien knew it was Sharlott, of course, and he aimed a curse her way as he collected his leather jacket and went out the door.

The morning of the afternoon Sharlott was to meet Simon, she had speed for breakfast and then went off to Kilburn High Road, where she bought a pair of red vinyl boxing boots at a charity shop. She had read somewhere that people tend to walk faster when they're wearing red shoes (instead of shuffling along in velvety grey ones), and she wanted them to serve as wings, if called upon.

Sharlott met Simon near Richmond Town Hall, where he insisted she have a tea especially blended for Richmond water. Then, unprompted, she began to complain about her writing—of the death-tinge inherent in weaving plots, of how it makes one an otherworldly kind of weary. She said she'd rather invest her life in drugs since they can love you back, while characters never can.

Simon shook his head as he glowered down into his tea. "So why do it?" he asked.

"Because," she replied, edgy and tender from slowing-down-speeding, "Because I don't want to die. I feel as if there's four deaths: one, when you're born;

two, when you surrender to your will; three, physical death; and fourth, when you're forgotten. If writing slows down that process, however minutely—then that's reason enough, if it can slow things down like . . . " She laughed. "Like ecstasy.

"Then again," she continued, "in some ways writing's like paying people to care. It's something I do because I'm too lazy to do anything substantial."

Simon reached across the table to take her troubled face in his hands. With her pale eyes and shaky pallor, she looked like an uncertain but avenging angel.

"Don't you see?" she pleaded to Simon. "How will we fill each day until night?"

"I don't have an answer," he said. "Unless you want to help me find Honor. That, what you just said, that's something she would say."

"Tell me one thing," Sharlott said as she pushed her plate of scones an arm's length away. "Do you live for her?"

"Yes."

Sharlott moved her head sharply from side to side, like an insomniac abed. "Then I'll help you if I can." She nudged his buckled shoes beneath the table with her red boot and sighed, relieved and devastated that he didn't love her.

Before they went to Simon's flat, they stopped at Dial House to hover momentarily by its blue and gold sundial, whose face promised it was redeeming the time.

Sharlott waited by the walk while Simon went inside his flat to retrieve what evidence he had of Honor: the same pictures and a postcard he'd shown before. He hoped that the things would take on a different context in the light of Sharlott's room.

Sharlott gazed at them, through them, as if they were negatives.

"I'm no mystery writer," she confessed, wishing she had copies of her books to prove it. "If anything, I write about people who, at crucial moments, daydream about others.

"Don't look at me like that," she continued, placing the pictures on a low table. "It's just books. They don't divine things or bring you love. In fact, they're not really good for much of anything. If I think of it, I much prefer art, going to museums and getting lost in the paintings. I'm that suggestionable—or empathetic."

"No one can save you there," Simon conceded.

When evening finally came they went to a club. A band, the Remember Me Nots, sang a song about having one foot in the grave and the other in the gutter, while Sharlott circulated in her fluffy-hemmed regal skirt which ended where her thighs began.

A friend of Damien's ran up to her.

"Regular fashion plate, you are," he said, his shiny bangs touching his lips. "Makes me believe you were born wearing clothes."

" 'Sex' that would be," added his friend, who embraced the boy's neck. "Bondage gear with the nappy. Suits baby best!"

"Is Damien here?" Sharlott asked either, both.

"No," replied the one with the fringe. "He hasn't been out much because he thinks someone is after him."

"Oh, he always pulls that," Sharlott said. "It makes him feel wanted. Honestly — his ego. Stinging like a centipede but with more legs."

"Ooh-ooh, lover's tiff," said the second boy as he steered his companion toward the dance floor.

When Sharlott saw Damien she paled. Before she could move, he pulled her to him and acknowledged her with a notoriously deep, dead French kiss. She broke away and motioned toward the bar, by way of saying she was there with someone.

"So that's it," Damien snarled, looking so horrible then as to be fantastic. "Remember this," he said. "Remember one thing. When you're in bed with him, with that way you have of holding off and then deciding to go along with it, make it seem your idea even . . . When you start getting into it and you're trying to show how you're so much more: in that instant, that best second right before you come . . . think of *me*."

Sharlott quickly found Simon and asked to leave. To be out in clubs was no longer fun, she insisted, it was worse than a dirge.

Simon asked who she was talking to, but Sharlott dismissed her boyfriend as a stranger, just someone who wanted to know the time.

"I want to go to your flat," she said, bristling live with the strange sex-current that is pure transference.

At the end of his bed, barely inside the netting and in line with his velvet-flat foot, Sharlott played for Simon. I'm drawn to you, she explained, because of our like-minded initials, their predestined symmetry. And how we're both looking for things without clues, searching sideways, almost.

"But I have a clue," Simon murmured. "I have the postcard, remember?"

"Oh, right, but still our search is our common lexicon. It's why I'm here." She stroked the toe of his shoe and Simon sat forward to meet her. He kissed her colorless cheek and she slipped out of her mock-royal outfit which, when it fell, landed stiff as a crown, with a domain of the floor.

Distractedly, Simon kissed her hair and her mouth, then reached back through the parted netting to the bedside table for a condom, which he put on as if it were a mismatched sock. Their sex was predictable and standoffish at first, but soon they nearly interred each other, their legs entwining like cemetery vines. Sharlott felt as if she were falling forever, like all was love and madness, and Simon used his hands like a conjurer.

It was then Sharlott saw the girl from Simon's photos. She appeared wearing a dress of white lace curtains, a wing of valances trailing behind her like a ghost-train. Honor took Sharlott's place beneath Simon, stretched out her ground-nest of deliberately

tangled black hair. When Sharlott saw Honor's pretty
face and soft blue eyes focusing far off and onto another, Sharlott cried out.

Simon made a sound like the swallowing of air and
then removed his rubber, observing a tiny speck of oc-
cult blood on the tip.

"Dead French letter," Sharlott said, abruptly taking
it from him and tying the end in a slip-knot. "That's
what my boyfriend calls them."

"Was he French?" Simon asked, put off.

"Italian, but more English. He grew up here."

"You met here?"

"Yeah. But we were apart for a long time. I had to
go back to America, so I would call him a lot. My day
would end while his began and so on, a seesaw, yin-
yang kind of thing. But we had a lot of phone sex,
which was really incredible long-distance. There'd be
this static pause to echo orgasm, an aching, cavernous
relay . . . "

Simon kissed her mouth, smothered and entered her
again, this time without protection. Sharlott considered the violence of the emotion—not the act—of
love, and she tried to use this knowledge to mute Damien's memory. But still it was his immaculate hard-
ness she felt, his protestations of love she heard. "It's
you who makes me come," he said, "and that's why:
love."

The next morning Simon helped Sharlott off to her
makeshift home, stopping long enough to question

her about her boyfriend. "I think he was that prole-turned-prat you spoke with in the club last night."

"No, no," Sharlott insisted, detailing instead the pop star whose face she'd seen on the t-shirt, on the tube-train, the day she'd met Simon.

"Now I know who you mean!" he cried. "But he's not even remotely Italian. Except for maybe his suits."

"Shoes," Sharlott corrected, kissing Simon good-bye. They held each other at arm's length, as if about to break into a spin. Slowly they assessed one another and labored to hide the awareness that they were just two people stuck saving places, marking time in the other's life.

In her rented room, Sharlott looked at a framed painting of flowers. It put roses where her cheeks should have been.

◻◼◼

The nearest florist to Sharlott was one that primari-ly served Brompton Cemetery, so Simon had to be very clear that the spray he'd ordered was for a girl, not a grave. He bundled the flowers in his arms (stems prodded his mat overcoat) and walked by the building site, dodging blotches of mud. He heard whistles and catcalls and looked up to see a gaunt construction worker perched high on a corner platform, his black hair edging out like his gargoyle's tongue.

In Sharlott's room Simon sat huddled on a vanity bench, grappling with ways he might bring up the subject of Honor. As usually befell him when he felt his most awkward, all he thought of was a token trip into nature.

"I . . . I was wondering if you might want to go camping," he shyly proposed to Sharlott. "I was thinking of this spot by Lock Wood, near Nuneham Park."

"I have no idea what you're talking about."

But he persisted, provided a touching explanation, and Sharlott sighed her agreement, asking only for a day to herself before they left.

◻▪▪

On a bitter Sunday morning she took several buses home to Gypsy Hill. The need to be near her writing was so strong that the gasping, crawling, convoluted Sunday service was merely a vague distraction. She thought instead of her pens, the duvet she'd sit on, the blank pages she'd finger like love.

She went up the walk, patted the lid of one of the garbage cans, and opened the door. The flat was so still she knew at once Damien must be out. She wandered into the den, saw a stack of videos he'd rented, probably long overdue. She unplugged the v.c.r. as if to silence its incessant graphic light, and then went into her writing room.

Nothing had been touched: it was like a tomb filled with records, magazines, toys, pens, and papers. A bowl was flooded with flower petals—they had surrendered there to float in sticky brown water next to

the computer, which was covered by a vintage ta-
blecloth.

Sharlott walked toward the soft daybed, but turned
back as if responding to an unwelcome question. She
walked down the hall, dreaming in daylight, to her
bedroom, to her wardrobe, where she kept copies of
her books in Doctor Marten shoeboxes. She pulled
out a couple, stuffed them in her purse. From the
hangers she plied holey Sex and Seditionaries, then the
more worse-for-wear Boy of London, and stashed
them in a carrier-bag. Purposely she left the dangling,
painted leather jacket, its heavy arms downcast.

Sharlott left the flat feeling old, as if her second
walk-through of youth were ended. She wished then
that she had a child onto whom she could impose her
self-longings, her furthest-lost dreams.

On the tube train back to central London, Sharlott
opened one of her books and read the first line. "To
know how very good I am, I have to run away," it
said, and she slammed the cover shut, as if it were an
unwelcome door.

◻◼◻◼

On the third day of their camp-out, Sharlott started
to resemble a Victorian gypsy — white lace, innumera-
ble scarves and shawls, hoop earrings. She and Simon
had gotten along, been close, and then tolerated each
other, except for once when he'd asked her what she'd
meant by something she had said.

Then, in the interior of their tiny tent, she had put her foot down. "When I explain things, I feel like someone else inhabits my body," she said, "and I hate it."

Sharlott put on a pair of round, tinted glasses and went outside to look at the fire. She needed to rinse out some cooking utensils, which she collected to take over to the tap at the edge of the campsite, adjacent to a gravel pit.

The weather was clear and warm as Sharlott walked across the field. She began to unravel chunks of aluminum foil for reuse, and as the water slid over the silver paper, she saw prismed in its surface the myriad reflections of a dark-haired young woman on horseback. The girl dismounted, then struggled to maneuver a wild-eyed baby who lolled papoose-style on her back. The child screamed like an irrational visitor barely on this side of life as the woman transferred the baby to the front of the red cloak she wore.

"Shh, Simonetta," the girl said as she comforted the child with a black woven blanket edged in elaborate tapestry. The baby's contorted face relaxed now, and revealed a cheek mole planted like a tiny asteroid on her page-white skin.

Sharlott dropped the foil and spun around to face Honor, realizing that her place, her circumstance in Simon's life, was doomed by Honor, Simon's one-love. It started to rain as the paper fell into a flash-puddle, and Sharlott turned to see no one, only erratic

designs made by wet rocks, colored and clouded by
her smudgy lenses.

She ran to the tent, threw off her shawls in favor of
her fuzziest Seditionaries sweater, and shorthanded a
note for Simon to read: "I m 1/2 sck o shadows."

Boarding a barge at Abbingdon Lock, a drenched
and wastrel-like Sharlott began her floating, unwaver-
ing journey back to London.

"Are you all right?" a man on the barge asked her.
"You look a damsel dead pale."

"I'm fine," Sharlott managed, despite feeling her
blood slowly freezing. The words for writing were
trapped in her mind now, stuck like curdled ink beneath a pin-prick.

From Richmond she took a taxi to Paddington Station, where she spent the night in a straight-backed
plastic chair. At the first train of morning, she boarded
the Circle Line for Victoria, and walked back to the
Tate Gallery.

The morning light was silvery and still as Sharlott
stood static in front of a painting that showed a young
woman drifting in a boat, wearing white and a pained
yet vague expression. Sharlott stayed there for a long
time, giving the picture her darkest peruse, until she
noticed someone standing near her.

"Shh," he said to her. He, of the Plague Deer Park,
of the Gargoyle Building Site, who looked like he was
from the Banshees. "Don't be afraid."

"I'm not afraid of you but of your shadow," Sharlott

replied, moving out of his line of influence. But he edged closer, eyeing her clothes.

"You'll be cool," he said, "you in your punk-rock jumper. You're one of us."

"I don't know what . . . "

"Shh," he said again, adding it just audibly. "Art Liberationists," he explained, and he produced a piece of paper that he safety-pinned to the shoulder of the girl in the painting.

"I'm off," he said. Sharlott didn't watch him go, but read the note instead. *Please look after this person,* it said. *Thank you. The Studio Rats.*

Sharlott walked a few steps to view a picture of arrows piercing flowers as two guards came running in, accompanied by the background sound of an alarm.

"Bloody Studio Rats again," said one, removing the note like a fat needle from thick-layered skin. "Bloody art libelists." Sharlott looked back and half smiled, feeling lighter and freer then than she'd ever felt.

Ad Astra
per Aspera

(To Heaven by Hard Ways)

C ross me," warned Ms. Hollywood Cemetery, "and I'll make you blot, an idiot in print. Also I'll kill you off, smother you in words as choking as Victorian nightclothes."

"Lie in fiction," he countered, "and I'll fix *you* like a stick-pin, in a song."

For their romance, it was a perfect beginning.

Ms. Hollywood Cemetery — a poet of, and out of, sorts — dispenses with pretense and lives in the graveyard. She's searching half-heartedly for the one who will die for her, looking distractedly for a thing more natural than love.

Miss Holly had been in love once, but then it had fallen out. It became clear the boy's love was nothing like hers and, in retrospect, the whole affair was scored with an emptiness she never hoped to really find again.

She lives in a tiny room two doors west of the cemetery gates, in the crevice of a flat-row street. Her home has a concrete yard trimmed with a barbed-wire picket fence. The holes in her ratted, rotted floor are patched with Ouija boards.

She composes pastiche poems on a manual typewriter, dreary words sucking shadows to cloud up the page. If she presses too hard, she chips her Biba black queen nail varnish.

Holly's lipstick, too, is a keyhole to anguish. Her long black hair's a timeline, falling out.

If friends should call, invite her somewhere, she usually declines. Her clothes won't darken their doors. But if she accepts, she spends the social time looking far off, the way recovering addicts are often lost to the present, focused on memories.

In the future, Holly is sure, everyone will be dead for fifteen minutes. Things will be better then.

☐■☐

This evening she walks to the cemetery in the fast-talking rain, toward the greater end when her body will turn to marble and she can consort with the other radiant white lies.

But until that time, she needs to be sidetracked.

For no clear reason she makes a detour to a clothing sale, to rummage through the moonlight bargain dumpster at a boutique called Despair's Psychosexual Thrill.

A glum sales assistant oversees the handful of dusky night-shoppers as they sift through an enormous metal trash bin of clothes. Churning in the bin are clothes made of delicate fabrics, graphically laddered and snagged. Minute flaws have grown into gaping cracks. Fishnets are particularly nasty: they stick to everything, especially shoppers' spiky, ornate jewelry.

Holly spots a maroon and black dress that she wants. When it's thrown her way by a disillusioned boy, she examines it, noting that the zipper is stuck. Never mind: she is so thin she won't need to use it anyway.

She goes to a card table to pay for her dress, deciding to take a cut in line proffered by a boy with overcooked purple hair. If Holly's distance vision were better, she would have looked right past him, failed to take in his lurid pop beads and the black kohl that forms jetties around his muddy eyes.

If she dreamed of boys at all, it'd be that they came in groups, with corsages tied to their wrists, a kind of daisy chain gang.

But this boy makes a remark about the moon, and how there are never any stars in the sky. It seems such a sad thing to say (she is yet to know of his predilection for speaking in pull-quotes), that she tells him she prefers viewing the moon through glass, anyway. "The moon through a window becomes an indoor moon, the way light through stained glass gets tainted divine."

"You must be an artist," the boy says, pursing his black-lined lips. "I'm Surfer Jay."

Holly nods a guarded reception, musing to herself that it would be easy enough to turn *surfing* into *suffering*.

"I'm Holly. Do you surf?"

"No, too dangerous. Too much pollution. I had a friend who surfed, used to surf by the power plant because the water was warmer near it. I think he's dead now."

"What do you do then?"

"Play hopscotch on Hollywood Boulevard. Play in a band called River Sticks. Design junk jewelry. T-shirts, too."

The sales clerk asks if they're ready to check out yet.

"They sell some of my stuff here," Jay says. "Inside. My line is called Malaprops. I have bell earrings with serpent tongues, and tiny gravestones with obscenities on them. Epitaphs."

"Okay," Holly says. "See you."

Holly goes home, to her bed which is a kind of glorified crib surrounded by an overwrought metal frame, like an infant's crypt. From her nightstand she takes out her binder—her bedside book of saints she's slept with. All told, the pages comprise a veritable Vatican Wax Museum. Holly locates the S's and slides her black index nail down them, bisecting Sebastians and Stevens, several S. J.'s, but no Surfers.

She pencils in his name as a possibility: *Suffer*, her name for him.

Holly sleeps in an antique slip, the straps of which fall to embrace her shoulders. But before she drifts, she prays, selecting a black and white rosary to help her roll and knead through the mysteries. She doesn't pray for things to change, or ask for rewards. She just thinks and talks, knowing that even the purest intentions can't alter anything, and that fate encompasses all—more than life, even. "Prepare for me," she suggests, trying to be helpful, "an early grave."

◻◼◼◻

The next morning Surfer Jay is as close to the beach as he's likely to get—long hot blocks from the sand, and then a huge stretch of lot and sand leading up to the water. Jay is in a clothing shop that has ordered his jewelry. He speaks to the clerk about buying the store's mailing list, and she gives him a form to fill out.

He goes back to his black woodie and finds that the side of it has been vandalized, spray-painted to read LOCALS ONLY. Jay moans his dismay—he would never go near their water. Brightening, he remembers he has glitter spray paint at home, which he can use to blot out this blasphemy.

Driving back to Hollywood he contemplates altering the graffiti to read LOCOS ONLY, or something else more suitable, but then he dismisses the thought, preferring to obliterate his awareness of such people rather than capitalize on their ignorance.

When his artistic task in the underground parking lot is completed, Jay goes out to a coffeehouse. By now, he has a glitter-confetti complexion that makes him stand out strikingly from the dowdier fixtures of the club, most of whom slouch like dusty potted plants.

That he would be at an espresso bar is an anomaly; but then, he felt like getting out, and since he doesn't drink, caffeine and sugar will have to do. Fortunately, Jay arrives before the doorperson, a muslin-clad harem kitten called Kate. It's unlikely Kate would have let Jay in—the bar, Paramania, allows her to reign with a policy of admitting people based not on their appearance but on their insight. Kate would have sized Jay up with one vertical glance: Kool-Aid hair, pancake makeup, embroidered overalls; he didn't have a chance against the people whose clothes look like the torn jackets of discarded books.

Jay sits restlessly on a threadbare couch, avoiding a slinky-like spring that threatens to assault, to pogo. Then he hears a scuffle at the door. He looks over his shoulder to see Holly in her maroon and black empire dress, arguing with Kate. "But I'm on the guest list!" Holly insists, explaining that tonight's poet (a girl named Claudia, who reads under the name of Cloud) has promised her that. Kate is unmoved from her Morris chair.

"We don't have a guest list," she spouts. "Who do I look like, Saint Peter?"

Holly is hurt; antagonism of any kind always makes her sad, renders her near tears.

Kate considers Holly's long black hair, her no-relief map of lipstick, her matte rouge. She thinks she knows who designed the dress. "Allow me to explain," Kate says. "If I let you in at all, it's because I deem you have insight."

"I always thought that what looks out, looks in," Holly answers softly.

"What looks out, looks in," Kate mimics, pausing. "I like that." So Holly walks in, into the waiting arms of Jay's sofa.

"You're the last person I'd expect to see here," she tells him.

"I could say the same to you, but I guess it wouldn't be true," he says, guiding her to sit while holding her cold hand in his lace-gloved one.

"Actually I've never been here before," says Holly, laughing now. "I came to see a friend read. Not that I'd ever read, myself; I think it's the outer limits of exhibitionism."

"You watch people read?" Jay says, too loud, a midway barker in a library.

"Shh!" she giggles. Not *watch* them read, *listen* to them."

"That's sick."

"I know," she admits.

"What was your name again?"

"Holly."

"Surfer J—"

"I know. I always call you Suffer in my mind, in the imaginary conversations I hold with you."

"I think that's a compliment," he says, meaning he's complimented that she thinks of him, but he doesn't get a chance to make this clear as Cloud lumbers her way toward a mock–Early American barstool, atop which she will sit and read, periodically swiveling to and fro in stark contrast to her words. Before she begins, Cloud lowers the shutters on the coffee bar just behind.

To Jay, Cloud's voice is a sonic blueprint of boredom, monotonous words from which he has to flee, in whatever way he can.

"I need to dedicate this piece to someone here tonight," Cloud says, but Jay isn't listening; he is daydreaming about carnival rides, especially one funhouse he recalls in which the mirrors were so rundown they offered no reflection at all.

"She's right out there," Cloud continues, Jay listening now. Cloud points. "Miss Hollywood Cemetery." Holly stirs, embarrassed.

"Now, Holly is a poet who'd never read, considering it an immortal sin of pride or something like that. But I prefer to think of reading as sharing, not hoarding."

Holly knows she is expected to storm out of the room, but it's Jay who leaps up like a jack-in-the-box, propelled by the sofa's errant spring. He retreats out of the shuttered, cluttered room, nearly taking down Astrid, an English girl he once knew. Astrid who'd told him "love" things didn't affect her, that it would take more than love to make it through the hedge-hewn maze that ended, enmeshed, at her heart.

It is the memory of Astrid that Jay shakes off as he walks the few blocks to his car. But when he is back inside his candy-colored apartment, he broods about Holly. When he heard her full name at the club, he'd asked himself, "Do I want her or do I not?" But it didn't matter: it was far too late to impose a rationale.

☐■■

Jay is up early the next morning, to work on jewelry designs. Stricken by a remarkable dearth of ideas, he decides to walk down Hollywood Boulevard and have breakfast at a nearby cafeteria. Detained in his bath-room, he rubs massage oil into his aubergine scalp — he'll wash the product out later in hopes that it will re-vive some feeling in the surface of his head.

He dresses in huge denim jeans that have stitched-on appliques of the planet Saturn. His shoes are thick-soled, like — he speculates — the layers of his skin. As a final touch, Jay fetches his yo-yo which he'll walk, like a pet, with him.

Hollywood Boulevard in the morning is smelly and still, much like a cellar rifled through by someone long gone. The few people about are homeless, runaways, or leftover musicians. A teen with a shaved head — the trail of hair that remains is coiled, poised—asks Jay if she can go with him, if she can stay with him. He says no, giving her what money he can spare.

After breakfast he peruses the t-shirt shops and dime stores that are beginning to stir awake. He wanders around thinking about things to design (he had an idea, but what was it?) and then heads for home, where he checks his mailbox. Inside the pint-sized metal vault he finds some folded sheets—a mailing list from yet another store, this one in Orange County.

In his living room he ruffles through the list, spying the names of a few friends, then is startled by the sudden materialization of Holly's. Miss Hollywood Cemetery shopping in *Orange County*? Maybe that was why she seemed so flighty, as if she were on the wrong side of the grave half the time. Her address he loves: Eleanor Street, not too far. He can visit her as soon as he's done with his hair.

The jar of Manic Panic color sits bright and inviting alongside the rest of his hair products. But his hair has kept its day-glo color, hardly faded at all, so he doesn't have to go another round with the dye.

☐■■

When Holly hears a knock she opens the tiny peephole and gazes out through serif grillwork.

"It's me, Suffer," Jay says, thrusting broomlike shards of his hair through the foot of the miniature door. "Rapunzel, Rapunzel, let in my hair!" he says in a high, clowning voice.

"Okay," she says, in black babydoll pajamas, over which she throws an ecclesiastical satin robe. Her feet are bare, save for black toenails.

"Hi," she says, admitting him and smiling right away at his t-shirt which reads "Is Nothing Scared?"

"I was just working," she continues, motioning toward her cardtable desk.

"I'm sorry—should I leave and come back?"

"No, that's okay."

"Can I see what you've been working on?" he asks, edging toward the table.

"No, not that. Here, you can look at this." She hands him a pamphlet bound in red construction paper.

Suffer leafs through it, sitting on her silent-age funereal bed, but the predominant effect her poems have on him is one of dizziness, from all the ***s and space breaks she employs. He feels most like he's been soundly thumped on the head.

"You might like this one better," she says, giving him a book called *Lost and Found*. He turns to a chapter called "Bells on a Hearse," and reads, aloud: " 'His eloquence a bubble / as fame should be.' That's really cool."

"It's not really mine, I just pretend it is. I got it out of a book, so it is mine now, in a way. Found poetry. No one remembers it, I'm sure."

Suffer sees something about a spider being a neglected son of genius and imagines a jewelry design. He scans the words "a dim capacity for wings/degrades the dress I wear."

"How did you find out where I live?" Holly asks.

"From Mini-Mal's mailing list. What were you doing out in Orange County? That's like being on the wrong side of the grave."

"I think that's a value judgment, don't you?"

"What, Orange County?"

"No, the other."

Suffer just shrugs, wants to kiss her flesh-colored lips. When he does, it's their first contact of the day — their lips meeting. He feels weak, leans Holly against the closet door. His hands inside her black robe encounter black lace, find tiny straps tied in taut bows at her shoulders.

She kisses his ear, his bell-tongued earrings duplicated.

Her robe is off, pajama bottoms drift down. Only her top remains, stubbornly knotted above and beneath her etched-glass breasts.

Suffer is out of his oversized jeans just like that. The only sound is when his crosslet and dogtag-linked belt hits the moldy wood floor.

Holly pulls the heavy spread off her bed and Suffer joins her there, though there's barely room for one. He fucks her with his fingers crossed because he doesn't want to lose her.

"Are those bats on your earring bells?" she asks him

later, mostly to wake him up so that she can move out
from beneath him and turn on her side.

"No, no, just scratchings. That's a good idea,
though."

"I *always* liked the idea of bells—the people, I
mean. The people who rang the bells. The Bell of
Saint Such-and-such. I don't think there are any now,
though. I think it's all done with tape recorders. No
people pulling ropes in musty tall towers . . . "

"I'm not sure," says Suffer. "I don't really know that
much about it. My parents were Catholic, but they fell
away from the church around the time I was born."

"You were the last straw."

"No, not like that. But, oh, you know . . . "

"Well said!" she laughs, hugging Suffer's thin torso,
her snake-charm bracelets ascending as she slides her
hands through the slots made by his arms.

Holly tells Suffer she's going to a carnival that night,
and once he's straight awake, he gives her a puzzled
stare.

"Usually I go to the cemetery at night, at dusk, really, to walk," she continues.

"Cool!"

"Well, I find I'm most content there, most alive and
in context and less . . . less vulnerable, I guess."

"Don't you believe in God?" he asks.

"Mmm, the carnival is put on by my church—not
my parish exactly, but I mean by the Catholic church.
So I kind of must. I do go to Mass, but my faith used

to be more traditional. It was more systematic. But then something happened."

"What?"

"It's minor, really. But I had this pair of glasses. They had black frames and were cat's-eye style, with rhinestones all along the brow-line like tiny eyes. I really loved those glasses. But one time during Advent I accidentally left them in the pew. And when I went back to get them, they were gone. And no one turned them in, either. So then at midnight Mass when I was looking at the Christmas crib, there was the baby Jesus wearing my glasses! I couldn't believe it! From that time on, it was as if my faith had been a sea of candles that were simultaneously pinched out."

"I don't get it," says Suffer. "I don't see why you didn't just reach in and get your glasses."

"Well, how could I? I mean, with all those people around? You can't just go climbing into the crib. Anyway, never mind. You don't have to understand."

"That's good," he says, getting up. "Because I'm totally lost. Besides, I always kind of preferred the devil myself."

"You do?"

"Yeah. In the way that he doesn't take responsibility for anything. He can't swim, either. Did you know that? The devil can't swim. That's why I call my band River Sticks."

"Now I'm the one who's lost."

"Just think of life as one long hayride with the devil. Only all the straw is damp." Suffer laughs.

□■■

There is a type of hayride at Dolores Mission's feast-day carnival. But it's only for toddlers, and it consists of plastic Easter-basket-grass-filled wagons pulled by what look like hooded monks. Most of the children are frightened and seem to view the friars as some kind of executioners.

The carnival is held in a corner parcel of East Los Angeles's Lincoln Park. The best way for merrymakers to get to it is to park their cars on a side street and then row little wooden boats across a man-made lake to the entrance. Suffer and Holly do this, drifting across the moat and leaving behind stucco motels, auto-wrecking lots, the concrete symbolizing the Los Angeles River, the County Hospital. They float wordlessly toward striped cotton-candy stands, a jeweled Ferris wheel, padded bumper cars, moonlight dancing beneath colored lanterns.

Even the sky's few mottled stars look like treasures, edged with clouds that are like bits of cotton from a gift box.

The two lovers lie back and let the boat make its own course in the musty-brown, velvet-algae–lined lake. Holly falls asleep as the tiny vessel lolls in the middle. She hears a woman's voice far off, singing what sounds like a hymn.

With Holly sleeping, Jay leans on the boat's crossbar and considers his career. He pictures it as a croquet-deck of moving cards. As the cards waltz closer, Holly stirs, hugs herself in her diamante-tinged black coat. Jay hears her say his name (the name she calls him) so he leans near her.

"I'm here," he tells her.

"Okay," she says. "I love you."

"Thanks," he replies, feeling like he's playing a game of word association at lover's leap. He feels warm, thinks his life might be a riddle with a kind of arbitrary diabolical or divine intervention, in which Holly has now announced her part. But he can't shed the fear that the two of them are just a pair of transient shadows living in the paradise of postponed assumptions, lush with the luxury of their own private imaginations.

"But cross me," Holly continues, rubbing her eyes awake, "and I'll make you a blot, an idiot in print."

Readied, Suffer hurls his defensive reply, as the boat juts up against the carnival shore.

⬜■ ■

In his apartment, at his drawing table, Jay madly designs. He works quickly, frantically, as if he's received a transfusion of mania. He applies Holly's poems like a thick coat of paint or mascara to his work.

He screens and colors t-shirts studded with bright pink spiders, the words "neglected genius" spelled out in glossy dewdrops on silly-string webs.

He makes one for Astrid, just so he can write Astrid Arachnid.

He creates jeweled sets: papalesque rings, earrings, and pendants using the plastic baubles that hold prizes dispensed from gumball machines. Inside each, he places little photos of his favorite famous people, limiting it to the ones who are articulate. So far, he has Bowie, Nick Cave, the Jesus and Mary Chain, Marc Bolan.

Last of all, he draws a dress for Holly. It's short, seedy, with two shoulderblade slats for removable wings.

When Jay arrives at Holly's house with his dress pattern, he notices she's done her nails poison-white, as though the tips of her bones were peeking through. Her thin legs are covered in bondage leggings that have a print of Gulliver being laced up by the Lilliputians.

"Who did those?" he asks, veering away, edgy.

"I don't know, I think Despair's . . . no, wait. You're not going to believe this, but I got these downtown, at a thrift store. St. Vincent de Paul's, in fact. They come from London, even. Don't ask me how they got here."

"I wish I thought of that design," he murmurs. "That pattern and all. I wish I did that. I've been working all morning, and up until now I thought I had a pretty good day."

Holly, miles off, excuses herself. In her bathroom she sits on the edge of her tub. After inserting her diaphragm, she rouges her labia. The smeared red goes down to her uppermost inner thigh where she writes, in eyebrow pencil, "please lie/deadlocked in me." She writes while Suffer sits on her bedpillow, thumbing through her bedside book of saints and through her pages torn out of poetry books.

Holly hopes the words will draw him in deep and forever. She enters the room unclothed, her sleep-walker's arms outstretched toward him.

"Do this for me," she says, aiming his face inside her legs. When he kisses her, the words get on his face like war paint.

"I can't die with you," he says. "And if that makes you think I don't love you, then you're wrong. The first time I ever had sex with you, you know what I did? I crossed my fingers." He shows her his hands and then places his clenched digits inside her. "This is how much I don't want to lose you."

When Holly ceases twisting, she pulls away. "You should have thought it through," she cries. "You should have thought how crossing your fingers works both ways, how it can mean you hope or it can mean you're lying."

Suffer gets up. "Goodbye," he says, using rose-petal rosary beads to bind her wrists to the metal headboard.

On his drive home, he makes a jeweled effigy of Holly, a gaudy jot of her sanctimonious self. That girl Cloud, he knows, will be his best customer.

◻■■

The phone keeps ringing and ringing, but Jay can't hear it from beneath his floral-print bubble hair dryer. When he finally answers, it's his bass player who tells him they have a show lined up. Jay wants a feather boa, the stragglier the better, to wear during the set. To look for one, he goes to the thrift store Holly told him about. On one of the wooden counters he finds an assortment of eyeglasses, among them a black cat's-eye pair. He buys the glasses, their myopic lenses scratched and blurred beyond repair. He can use these, he knows. He can use the pieces of double-glazed glass to make jewelry orbs, beneath which his planets might move less encumbered, like royalty.

The
Jealousy
Loan

*a*t the death-lingerie party, something is amiss: all the bustiers and girdles, each wail-bone in-seam and garter, are a ruddy shade of puce, of fresh-faced peach, or vitamin-happy tangerine. Simonetta pinches her eyes shut, thinks the vision a result of her unendingly long late nights. But when she looks again her dreams are confirmed, lightened. Tufts of harvest-gold shag carpet edge the g-strings lovingly arranged on the floor.

Not the type to linger over Tupperware martinis or dwell amidst the coffee klatch, Simonetta merely wants to imprint her presence on the group and then move quickly from their clutches—to be that breathlessly missed.

A woman in patterned chiffon asks Netta where she's from, originally. Simonetta smiles that she doesn't know, that she was plucked up in her baby carriage by a North Dakota tornado and than planted, intact, two blocks away. "But what happened while I was in the air is anybody's guess," she explains.

"Oh, I see," the woman replies, bored now. "Because I thought you were English."

▫▪▫▪

The Jealousy Loan is kind of old, but still he holds up, wielding his way on his morning walk through Brompton Cemetery. He's never been too dumb to recognize love, only too lost to articulate it.

He'd like to sit on a stone bench for a moment, but opts for the grass instead. The rest is brief, though, for when he sits still, he petrifies.

Suddenly mobilized by a stunting fear of irrelevance, he considers where to go next: he'd leave for Berlin, but it's not the same now. Better, more decadent, to return to America.

▫▪▫▪

In the changing-room mirror Simonetta observes the beauty mark on her bond-white cheek, puts on her tapestry cloak, and primps to leave the party without, of course, purchasing the March-violet garter belt she's stashed in her heart-shaped satchel.

▫▪▫▪

The Jealousy Loan looks good, like someone used to living off others' sorrows. He's comfortable on the plane, thinks of the clouds as oatmeal, thick with angels. The world beneath is a paradise lost, because people take it up.

Primarily, he's a resurrection man, a boy who really doesn't like girls but subsists on his capacity to fulfill them. He starts by standing in, to make their boyfriends jealous, until the inevitable happens and the girls fall madly in love with him.

It's then that he asks to borrow money, usually for clothes, and takes flight.

The day before, in the March Hair salon in the Fulham Road, he'd done just that. Demona, a soft-eyed stylist with hair the color of sloe gin, believed her world ended and began in that upstart minute when she knew she loved him. So she raided the cash register to come up with a deposit on a cozy flat in Pimlico, a place which Andy (The Jealousy Loan) can now see speck-sized from the plane.

But Andy doesn't always get off scot-free. At times it's quite the reverse, and he's caught dwelling on a previous girl's writhing skills or a particular piece of her clothing. Still, he's sufficiently protected from excessive grievous harm by way of his candy-box heart, lined as it is with perlitic, prefab corrugated cardboard.

"What inspires you?" Demona had asked at a rooftop garden party in Kensington.

"Your clothes," Andy replied, edging her toward a shuttered balcony just within her boyfriend's radius. He kissed her there and then they had druglike sex against the unusually rough night sky.

Right after he's left a girl Andy has the temporary, presentient conscience of a displaced ghost, and worries how he'll stay aloft. He knows the sex he gave them was a kind of shorthand, a white voodoo. And he also knows that what's missing from his girls' lives are the things they'll never have.

"May he rot in a shallow grave," Demona says, forced to pay back her salary advance in endless complimentary haircuts given to scruffy models baited by flyers in the vicinity of Earl's Court station.

◻■◻■

Simonetta's words have an expatriate's etch, although to her mind she's never been out of the country. "Tell a lie," she'll eventually say to Andy, in tones of disbelieving British vernacular. He'll be only too happy to comply.

Netta has long, ringleted hair and fingernails the shapes of planchettes. If she loves at all, she loves in anger, an orphan's mode. About her father it didn't matter, but it was her mother Netta was concerned with, having pale recollections of a woman placing her in the center of a dozen eggs, which served as a playpen. Netta remembers crawling, moving, pointing her tiny arms like clock hands. She's certain that her mother is the same age as herself; doubts that she was successfully born. No, a part of her life is stuck somewhere.

She still hears her mother's lullaby:
Treetop cradle rocks
in and out of time
little girl lost
you're not mine

fall forever, feel
the depth of hollow

extract grey sorrow
for your netted bed

hush in sleep, let me
drop tiny appledreams on thee

And the song, like a riddle, gifts Netta with sleep-lessness.

❑■■

Once Andy has established himself in a Hollywood hillside snug, he starts thinking ahead to future months' rent. His landlord, Shelley, is a possibility: what he knows so far is that she is a psychologist with a small, insistent dog called Emp. Shelley sees clients in a portion of the old, mock-Tudor house she now shares with Andy. The people come into the cold, tiled hallway to be quickly ushered toward the study, a beveled, bedeviled room with casement windows often clawed by shrubs in the outside relief.

Andy has his own room, furnished with a bunkbed that is evocative of cowboy and Indian sheets and moth-spotted plaid blankets. Shelley explains that she'll undo the beds for him but Andy smiles, shyly and slyly assuring her he'd see to that later. For now he'd prefer to lie on the bottom one, with the upper berth a canopy of mattress-stuffing clouds and box-spring tornadoes.

◻▪▪

Simonetta lives in Silver Lake, in a guest cottage she calls Temperate House for the way it's almost hermetically sealed. She has vases and plants and temperature control, humidifiers and capsule-shaped pillows to envelop her head. She has silence, but no deep sleep.

Her adoptive parents still support her, would welcome her back whenever she wishes. But Netta's not tempted or inspired by the memory of Fargo, of Northport Shopping Center, or of a hauntless downtown of Depression-era boarding houses long since leveled to be replaced by nothing at all.

She'd left North Dakota as soon as she was physically able (that is, aged thirteen) to head for Los Angeles, climate of the shiftless and other preoccupied explorers. Back then, Netta lived just north of Chinatown, sharing a room with other runaways attempting Los Angeles punk-rock. They missed the heart of things by years and miles, in the way only migrants can. Still, Netta saw her share of sex-streaked, sex-starved alleys, of the cloying courtyard that held Madame Wong's and the Hong Kong, of the Atomic Cafe, until punk gasped out and fluttered spirally into early gloom. But gloom, too, soon went all sinister and creepy—a So-Cal goth tale of incest and deceit.

Which is why as she lives now, she lives in seclusion.

When she dresses, what she wears is slightly past-tense, a lesson she learned. She knows the value of doing things a little out of time, a fraction off-speed. Bright colors at Bauhaus, a prim cashmere sweater with bondage pants, effortlessly separates an original from a cult-crawler.

◻◼◻

The next morning Andy puts on a cloak-and-dagger–printed bathrobe and heads downstairs for the breakfast nook. At the foot of the stairs stands Emp, yapping emphatically. The dog may be well-groomed, thinks Andy, but beneath that shiny coat is nothing more than a tangled nest of nasty nerves.

"Emp, come here," calls Shelley. "Don't be so petty." She laughs at what she thinks is her pun, and points it out to Andy when he appears in the doorway.

"What can I get you for breakfast?" she asks.

"Oh, you don't have to go to any bother," he answers, relieved. She will be a pushover, a pawn, in the palm of his plans.

Over coffee and cinnamon toast, Shelley tells Andy

of her upcoming weekend, of her on-again-off relationship with her boyfriend, a probation officer named Darren.

"This weekend will take the cake," she explains, pouring more coffee for him, for herself. "We're supposed to be going to a Roaring Twenties Picnic in Wattles Park. It's a wonderful event, really, a real period piece of living theater, put on by a local group called Hollywood Heritage, of which I am a member. Come to think of it, you should attend. In fact, you must! You can come as my guest."

"But you were saying about Darwin," Andy says, deliberately mistaken.

"Oh, he'll be there," she replies. "That's one thing we know for certain. He'll be there."

□■□

In the early morning Netta is still wearing the previous day's clothes: bloomers and a cable-knit yachting sweater. Sleep was so remote she'd never removed her French-heeled pumps, which stretch out in front of her as she watches movies until dawn.

The feature is *Our Dancing Daughters*, a kind of flapper epic from the period. Joan Crawford embodies Flaming Youth, but to Netta she's Netta herself and her mother—one dancing, the other a shiny piano reflection. But it's Netta's mother who is obvious in the frantic Charleston step, the waving fringe, and most of all, in Crawford's pool-deep eyes that assure of an impending Peg Entwistle–style Hollywood Sign high-dive into the alternately arid and lush landscape of despair.

Netta thinks about a notice she'd seen at the market, a program for a 1920s picnic. Might her mother be there, floating airlessly in a tea dress, a hand-beaded purse brushing against her drop-waisted hip-bone? Netta looks nearer back and remembers a boy named Mario, whom she knew back in her China-town days. He would have made the perfect date for the picnic, considering his slick black hair and asymmetrical dimples, but he died several years ago.

Netta didn't love him, and at that time Mario had not wanted a girl. But he was so aloof she always felt safe with him. She shifts her position on the sofa, the better to fall back. The past drifts in, in slow motion the way it always does: absurd, really, considering that what happened went by so quickly.

Mario could be her date regardless, Netta decides. She could conjure him easily—he'd be as memorable as any nodding companion. He could lightly take her hand, shield her from direct sunlight, and give that moody look he'd still be trying to perfect, even from across the bar.

With the money Shelley has apportioned for him to buy a suit for the picnic, Andy heads for Melrose Avenue, only to be waylaid by Hollywood Boulevard. Here, he realizes, he could buy something and be able to eat lunch, too. In a shop, Enmity [For Men], he's attended to by two girls, Organdy and Antagony, who are twins via their aubergine hair and contrastingly pierced noses. They pet Andy, display the shop to him, lead him into an alcove called Lolligag Gifts. "Pranks to linger over," Antagony explains, clicking on a set of attached commemorative bracelet. "They unlock with a venerated skeleton key of the corresponding saint, only I'm not sure how it goes," she says, scowling now as she tries to slide them off.

"Suffer!" she yells, startling Andy, who perceives this as being out of the character he has imposed on her. "Suffer, help! I can't get this fucking thing off!"

A boy appears on the balcony. He has the same royal hair but his eyes are obscured by tortoise-shell glasses.

"Check the manual," he yells down. "Look it up in the Ten Commandments. How the hell should I know?" When Suffer spots Andy, he clears his throat.

"Pardon me," he continues. "I didn't know they were helping you. Let me know if you see anything you don't need." Suffer descends the spiral staircase dramatically; it wobbles slightly from where it's anchored to the ceiling. Once he's close enough, he offers his black-nailed hand to Andy.

"I'm Jay," he says. "I own this shop. The chicks are just here for decoration. I mean, they're supposed to help people, but sometimes I think they're more of a distraction than anything else." He shrugs. "Chicks. Glam chicks. Gloom chicks. Punk-rock chicks. Death chicks." He shakes his crayon head. "Anyway, can I help you?"

Andy tells Jay about the party and Jay produces a black linen bondage suit. He asks Organdy to throw in a "Pashion is a Fashion" undershirt, which she retrieves, along with a diamante-patterned bow tie. She puts the tie around Andy's starch-white neck and Suffer suggests Andy might like to wear her instead.

"Fuck you, boss," Organdy says and walks away.

"The tie is vintage," Suffer says. "Clothes are like wine, you know. And speaking of whine: Organdy!"

"What?" she responds, peeking over the counter she'd been hiding behind, eating a french-fry lunch with Antagony.

"Write him up, will you? Andy, was it? Well, keep in touch, Andy. Let me know how you make out at the mad tea party. Who knows, I may even go myself. What do you think, girls?"

But the girls have sunk down again, immersed in an MTV soap opera.

"Chicks," he says.

"Birds," shrugs Andy.

As Suffer Jay goes back upstairs, the girls discuss Andy's potential. "One thing's for sure," says Antagony. "With him it's a clear case of who'll get the last cry."

"Dingy—my favorite color!" says Organdy as she opens a cardboard crate. "But who order all these day-glo briefs? They're hideous! But then again," she pauses to pout. "I guess one has to consider the topic it covers." And then she laughs cherubic, a baby-faced demon.

◻◼◼

Andy stays the right distance from Shelley's side—just inside wraparound arm's length. He's yet to be paraded before Darren but is relieved that Emp was turned away at the gate. "Ridiculous!" Shelley had fumed. "Why, he's even been to Vertigo with me."

So Andy had driven Emp home, placed him in the passenger seat of the rented touring car. Each time he rounded a corner, Andy considered easing the dog right out the door.

Andy fetches Shelley a second glass of champagne, but graciously declines her suggestion that they do an interlocking toast. "I don't know you that well," he sighs.

When he goes to replenish his plate of cucumber sandwiches, he spies Simonetta, who's wearing cotton lace from the 'teens plus stultifying flesh-colored platform shoes. He falls in love with the breeze made by her hand-embroidered skirts; he is drawn in by the presence that softly clings to her like faded sachet. In short, he is felled by Mario.

Andy moves closer to Netta, momentarily forgetting his duty toward Shelley. He walks on grass made up of tiny green rosebuds which he squashes with his Doctor Marten boots. The lawn can't possibly spring back.

"Hello," says Netta, tentatively leaning onto Mario, who's more like a sliding bannister. Within three sentences, she and Andy arrange to meet, and

Netta knows it's like making plans with the devil: he'll never cancel, and if he alters the plot it'll only be for the common bad.

Their sex, too, when it happens, will be as tedious as a run-on sentence, and every bit as desperate.

Throughout the remainder of the afternoon, Andy gets progressively more drunk, uncharacteristic of him. By the time he's ready to escort Shelley home, she questions his sobriety. "It's okay," he assures her. "When I'm like this, I can drive better than I can walk."

Nonetheless, Shelley opts to leave with Darren and his disgruntled date, providing Andy with the money to take a cab. "What about the car?" he asks, but she waves it off, telling him they'll arrange for it to be picked up later.

But he has the keys so Andy drives the touring car up into Coldwater Canyon, reversing Montgomery Clift's fateful trip. He's heard that a death mask of the actor's original (pre-accident) face clings to the telephone pole his car collided with; that it's best visible by car headlights in the fog.

Andy reflects on his favorite Monty films: *The Heiress, A Place in the Sun.* Thinking of *Raintree County*, he considers growing sideburns.

He wanders the car back into the gully of Los Angeles and ends up at Du-Par's Coffee Shop in Farmer's Market, where he has to refuse tea and insist on coffee, for the waitress thinks he's English.

"If anything, I'm Canadian," he tells her, and she is so charmed she brings him a cheese danish, gratis.

"Nine, thirty, fifty-five," a girl in the booth behind whispers into Andy's ear. Impossible, undesirable measurements, but she has a refined voice so he turns his head toward her anyway.

"That's the date James Dean ate his last meal here, before, you know . . . " She twirls an onion ring around in a flat bowl of French onion soup. Her pink lipstick is on the edge of the bowl, on the straw of her iced tea, and a trace remains on her tiny mouth. She's accompanied by two other girls but Andy doesn't bother to sum them up; they're of no use to him.

"I never really liked James Dean," he answers. "Too pouty and manic for my taste. And two opposite elements cancel out anyone in my book." He gets up to leave and when he arrives home, he's alone.

In bed he spins, stares up at springs that asterisk Netta's hair. He imagines he's in a train compartment circumferencing Lake Geneva with her.

◻◼◼

The next day in Enmity, Antagony and Organdy are wearing matching yellow bugle-bead sheaths that have tattoo-splotches of lace dangling past the hems. Organdy sits, intent on stringing alphabet beads to the shoelaces of her patent leather monkey boots.

"Lucille," she says and spells, because that's what she wants to call her shoes.

Suffer Jay appears around noon, and Antagony interrupts viewing her soap to ask him how the Gatsby party was.

"Search me," he says. "I stayed upstairs in the old house the whole time."

"Was that guy there?" asks Antagony.

"She means Andy," assists Organdy.

"Yeah, I guess. You chicks have your beady blue eyes on him?"

"Antagony thinks he could give her a good time. I myself always have a good time because I never care what I do."

Antagony leaps up to answer the phone, snarling the hem of her dress on an earring tree she'd neglected to place on the check-out counter. "Suffer, my dress!" she shrieks. "I need another one."

"Help yourself," he smirks. "It all comes out of your salary."

While Antagony grimaces, inwardly she smiles to herself, picturing the walk-in closetful of items she's ordered for the store and then spirited away, boxes and all, to her home.

"I'm surprised you like Andy, Antagony," says Suffer. "I thought you only went for those ghostly boys, the kind who look like they should be pushing up daisies."

"That's *why* I like him," she answers. "He wouldn't push up the daisies. He'd pull them right under with him."

■■■

A bowl of oranges gleams on the kitchen table in Temperate House. The pure sunlight tints and tickles the bone-china teapot that, taken out of its woolly house-shaped cozy, Simonetta tilts into her precisely-patterned teacup.

Twin lumps of sugar bob like rafts in her tea as Netta looks down, despondent. Her mother remained invisible yesterday, when Netta was so sure she would show herself. Netta oars her teaspoon, reflects at length on what she imagines is her past.

When they were as mother and daughter, Netta remembers pretending that her mother didn't exist.

"The usual thing," Netta muses now. "I was inspired by someone I essentially ignored."

But really Netta's memory is blocked, and she can feel it like a candy-cluster headache. She can see her mother clearest, with the most ease, when she's picturing her as an age-mate, the way she generally figures in her reminiscences.

Her mother was called Honor and she had a mass of black hair that she combed like the funnel-cloud of Netta's infancy. Honor would sit in a bay window and repeat, "Oh, to fall off the face of the earth!"

So maybe she went to Europe?

Or Scotland or Wales?

Honor had told Netta that life would be easy for her, "pretty (as she was) as a (paint-by-number) picture." But Netta never feels pretty—she just feels cheated and cursed, for how could she base her life on beauty when she herself never experienced it?

Today Netta decorates her rooms with only antique mirrors, ones that are mottled with carbon clouds and are completely effective at rejecting reflections.

Andy, hung over, slips out of the house by now presumably occupied by Shelley and Darren. Emp is nowhere to be found; perhaps he's cradled in bed beneath Shelley's curled feet.

He takes a taxi to Netta's home and is so sickened by the unsavory ride that he nearly goes back to collect his things and leave for London, for anywhere. But he presses on and locates Temperate House.

Netta answers the door in a horizontally side-split Alaia skirt and a cheerleading sweater crewel-stitched with a large black *A*. It's hard for Andy to guess if the *A* stands for adultery or the more traditional anarchy. He can hope.

For a moment Netta sees herself in Andy's eyes but she quickly averts her gaze. She could probably out-stare anyone, if she desired eye contact.

Netta is not comfortable with Andy the way she is with Mario. Still, he has a common tenuousness that she finds reassuring.

And it's even odder for Andy: there's nothing self-serving about his knowing Simonetta, and she hasn't enlisted him for any purpose; there's just this vacuum/reverse-aura draw.

Andy places his index finger on Netta's pale lips,

gives her crosses for kisses. She wants not to see him then and will have to make him go away.

So Netta starts to tell him about her mother and leads him down the hall to show a framed photo.

"Don't you have any respectable mirrors?" he asks suddenly.

"No."

"Is that a Nosferatu kind of thing?"

"Not really, although I suppose everyone has considered themselves to be something of a vampire at one point in their lives. But no. The day the dead walk, I want to be out, lost among the ghosts. I'm not that much of a goth."

"Me neither," Andy smiles. "And it's a good thing, too. They would have run me out of England even sooner, had I been."

"You lived in England?"

"Yeah, all over, really. I was what you call ex-directory."

"Because my mother lived in England, London," Netta continues, showing Andy a picture of two young people at Stonehenge, the man looking the most apprehensive. The woman is pretty, slight—at once Victorian and spent with twentieth-century gloom. She could be from La Belle Epoch, she could be from last year. She is a 1920s shadow or a sequence of the swinging sixties. But the man with her is as current as postage.

"Who is this?" Andy asks, aiming at the man.

"I don't know. He could be my father or he could

not be. I do know he was superstitious about having his picture taken."

"Well, I can see why. Because there's another picture aging in an attic somewhere! Netta, I waited on this guy in the Black Letter in Fulham Road less than a month ago. I'm sure of it!"

"Hmmm," says Netta. "But what about her?" Her finger leaves a moonprint on the glass.

"Her I don't know about. But him, I'm telling you. There's something really strange going on here. If these are really your parents, then there must be some pictures in an attic somewhere."

"Why do you keep saying that?"

"Because I'm telling you I just saw that guy!"

Netta doesn't understand Andy's confusion. Faith and time, for her, have always been little more than a cosmic game of leapfrog.

"This is too weird for me," he says, throwing up his arms like drowning. "I've got to get away for a while. I'll call you later this evening. Don't take it personally —I just need time to get over this."

"Concentrate on the girl," Netta calls down the porch stairs after him. But before too long he's in Enmity, certain that the *A* on Netta's sweater foretold Antagony.

"And I am neither a dweller among men nor ghosts," Antagony recites for Andy. Organdy, overhearing, shrugs and says, "That's true. What she prefers is a hybrid of the two."

"Don't look at me," says Andy. "That's definitely

not me." Then he places himself in Antagony's violet eyes.

Antagony is prevented from leaving Enmity early because a customer—a spiral, spectral reflection known as Skitz—has entered the store. He wants to buy a harmlessly dated pair of letter-sharp pointy boots, and Antagony has to go deep into the back stock to find them. She returns, brandishing them in their tiny pine box.

After Skitz leaves, Organdy emerges from behind a triptych standing mirror. "I hid because I thought you'd probably want to wait on that guy."

"No way," Antagony says, hitching her thumb in the direction of Andy. "I hate that cobwebby kind of guy. Let's get out of here," she says, going over to Andy.

"Remember, I'm in tonight," Organdy calls after them. "So don't get any ideas about coming home." Then she adjusts the snood that restrains her fanlike ponytail.

As they drive away in Antagony's shiny car, Andy plots how he will lose her. She wants to go to the movies to see *The Cat Mummy* and as they take their places in the boat-shaped theater, Andy feels ill, as if he's in an ark filled with pairs of identical people, headed smack for eternity.

He goes up for popcorn and exits the theater. Another guy takes his seat; to Antagony, his sweaty hands are indistinguishable from Andy's in the theatrical gloom.

As Andy takes a cab to Shelley's, he rehearses his explanation. Because she was with Darren, because the house was so still, because he couldn't find Emp . . . He knows just how much to say: his built-in mechanism for equidistance is an effortless occupational advantage.

When he arrives, he finds Shelley downstairs, on the sofa and in playdeck loungewear. She starts when she hears his stories, interrupts to enlighten him about her theory of central love, which stems from a core, a stick-impaled avocado heart.

Noisily she shows Andy a note she'd prepared for him, in case he returned while she was away or in session. "All love," read its complimentary closure, "and not too much madness."

Andy feels as if he ought to ask about Darren but by now he knows his destiny. He has memorized it like a creed, a trip-proof concrete schoolyard rope-rhyme.

As he advances to take Shelley's hand, the housekeeper enters the room. She carries Emp's satin pillow, with its turreted tassels dangling at the corners. Missing from the pillow's center is Emp, who would usually be placed there, curled like a ring and biding for Shelley's glimmering admiration.

"I can't find him, ma'am," the housekeeper, Desde, says, faux–old-worldly.

Shelley panics and grabs her car keys from the roll top desk, retrieves her Burberry coat from the hall closet. She reenters the room, still in her mules, and instructs Andy to stay close by the phone in case there's any news. "On Emp's collar," she explains, "well, it's a Chanel collar, but that's beside the point. On it is a device, an attachment that holds money and a note that reads 'Have dimes, can't dial.' Maybe someone will respond to that."

Andy nods, imagining how he'd react. Besides, Emp would never let a stranger — or even an acquaintance — near him. Then Andy smiles as he pictures the dog lost as a bottle in the ocean, with that tiny scroll-note a waterlogged string of seaweed.

Back in his room Andy sits on the lower berth of his bed, the upper reaches of his hair grazing the box springs and looking like faraway rain. He lies back, his feet jutting off the bed, and places his arms like wings at his head, assuming the dream position.

He thinks of Netta and is nervous as to how he could have fallen in love with her. Girls to him have always been assignments, even the ones he may have loved. But what is this piercing thing? It couldn't be her borderline-pretty face or her clouded skin . . . it's what he can only define as her deeper length, a thing he has never encountered before.

But he knows she has to be a little bit off, considering she thinks her mother is in a photo of what is obviously a pair of Netta's friends vacationing in England. As Andy pictures the photo, he suddenly remembers who accompanied the man when he was in the Black Letter. It was a woman, that washed-up mystery writer called Sharlott who made a name for herself by dating pop stars. Andy scowls his disdain. He recalls the woman perfectly now, especially since it was she who signed the bill.

Andy rushes to call Netta.

◻◼◻▨

Emp is found at Lake Hollywood, a reservoir. Damp and shivering, the dog has slipped beneath the chain-link fence only to be chased by a stringy young coyote, who was distracted from stalking a mockingbird. The coyote, in turn, was rattled by a man dispensing algae-killing chemicals into the water supply.

Emp wasn't exactly forced into the lake—he was just scared shiny. Plus he'd never seen a creature as ungroomed and uncivilized as the coyote. But a worker managed to corner the tiny dog betwixt bramble and barbed wire. He picked him up with gloved hands; Emp had seldom felt a fabric so rough, and he trembled and twisted and nipped as the man carried him to the hillside office. Then the man dialed the number he found on the dog's collar.

His rescue message is an unobtrusive, static handclap on the call-waiting line, ignored by Andy as he initiates his conversation with Netta.

"Where are you?" she asks, curious about the castanet clicks.

"I don't know where I am unless I'm with you."

"That's silly."

"Well, how do you feel about me?"

Netta pauses, long. "Let's just say I feel the same

about you as you do about me." She thinks this is a fail-safe reply.

"Oh, fantastic! When can I see you?"

"What about your job? And your girlfriend?"

"It's not really my girlfriend."

Andy signs off and then prepares a note for Shelley, explaining carefully and in detail how he's gone to search for Emp.

When he arrives at Netta's in the long-overdue rental car, Netta is wearing a Gaultier Junior jacket and Catholic schoolgirl skirt, hiked up to show the tops of her black fishnets. On her feet are high-top canvas basketball shoes.

She rubs her eyes.

"Were you asleep?"

"I don't sleep much."

"Say, Netta, show me that picture again. I think I may have remembered something."

When she brings it, Andy realizes for certain that the woman he remembers is not the one portrayed in the photo.

"I remember who this guy was with now," he says. "And it wasn't her. It was this kind of pathetic writer."

"Do you think she knew my mother?" Simonetta cups her hand over her heart in an act of glee.

"She knew this guy, that's for sure. At the time I thought it was funny because he was a nobody, and she had a reputation for bagging rock stars."

"How do you mean?"

"I mean she used them to achieve her notoriety. She

was like a modern-day groupie. Like 'I'm with the Damned.' "

"I thought the groupie thing died along with Nancy Spungen."

"Well, you're wrong. What are fans but groupies?"

"Fans don't have sex with the stars."

"It'd be better if they did," laughs Andy. "That way they'd get over it."

"Oh, I don't know," says Netta softly. "I think thwarted sex makes for the best pornography."

Holding her shoulders, Andy sits Netta down next to him and when he kisses her thigh, one of his earrings gets ensnared in her fishnets. He tears free, leaving a heart-snag in the diamond pattern as Netta rolls her skirt another notch and struggles out of her high-waisted cotton underpants.

When Andy removes her Gaultier jacket, Netta gets up to retrieve it from the floor and then drapes it life-like around the armchair.

Then she unbuttons Andy's floral blouse, unflies his 501's.

In her roseate bedroom, on sheets the color of warm milk, their bodies align and malinger.

"I love you," he announces, from over her.

"You *do?*" she wonders, sitting up.

"Sometimes," he says, and his shoulders rise to meet the length of his hair.

When it's clear their sex is over he traces the letter *A* on her flat chest with his accusing finger. *A* for effort, though it's clear Netta is never there. A protective, guardian glow surrounds her, a shiny, filmy sheath, a plastic cling-wrap shawl. It covers her body like the sheen of a drowning victim, and Andy knows now that this barrier is most of what compels him.

Netta doesn't sleep and she stirs so much that Andy is likewise prohibited, so he tells her he believes the people in the photo she'd given him a copy of can't possibly be her parents.

"Not him. Her!" Netta reminds.

"Netta, they're too young."

"This isn't fair of you."

And she orders him out, leaving Andy perplexed at his laxity, appalled at his newfound propensity for saying exactly the wrong thing. It's as if in her presence his former abilities are as lifeless as plastic dandruff-snow in a broken holiday dome.

Simonetta gets up and puts on a satin slip that droops like sorrow, and a Navajo blanket bed jacket. She leaves a wilderness trail of tissues between her bed and a bookshelf, where she keeps her mother's scrapbooks.

She selects the one that has a traffic light on the cover, a semaphore of amber and lunar-white hanging mid-street. Netta observes the book somberly, as she would a tornado watch.

Her adoptive parents had said her mother once saw a classical concert in Bismarck and from then on wanted to be an artist. But Netta thinks this story has to be a joke; it didn't fit her any more than their insistence that Honor aspired for Netta to be Miss America.

Then, too, there was a musician whose career her mother followed, but the pages about him are missing from the notebooks now: only ragged curbs of paper remain in the metal margins.

Netta pauses. Could her mother have been the woman Andy saw in London, even though he said it wasn't? All the pieces seem to fit. Was he just lying to sidetrack, to trick her? To keep her from what she wants?

◻◾◼

Shelley is orchestrating a homecoming party for Emp, and she busily prepares his favorite goose paté. When Darren arrives, he starts to assemble a doghouse that looks more like an ancestral home. Georgian ghosts could glide down its staircases; prisoners might rattle in the towers. Red and blue ribbons curtain the hallway.

Darren begs off staying for the actual celebration, especially once Andy arrives, windblown and flustered with the invention of where he's been.

"It's okay, Andy, it's okay!" Shelley interjects. "Emp's here! He's back!"

But Darren is skeptical, disgusted. The boy uses for sure, and it's just a matter of time until he uncovers What. He takes his leave, receives a staged kiss from Shelley, and grunts his farewell to Andy.

"I should say goodbye to Emp," he adds, through

his teeth. "But goodbye doesn't seem right for a homecoming."

"He'll understand," says Shelley, turning her back toward the kitchen. "Desde is grooming him now, anyway."

After Emp has nibbled his paté, nipped at Andy's heels, and gobbled Shelley's attention, the dog runs several final circles and then collapses, exhausted, on the cool marble floor of his new home.

"The house is a replica, to scale, of the home where he was bred," Shelley explains. "I was waiting for his birthday to present it to him, but I thought somehow that today was the right occasion. It's all in hopes that he'll never leave again—that it'll provide a kind of genetic memory for him."

"Well, I can't speak for him, but if I was reminded of my home, I'd run like hell," Andy says.

"Andy, where is home for you?" Shelley tilts her head in concern.

"Victoria. But I was born in Newcastle."

"This is your home now," Shelley insists, to circumvent his story. "Would you like another drink?" She moves unsure, like the champagne.

They toast, to homecomings.

"Speaking of which," says Andy, "the touring car is still outside. Shouldn't I return it?"

"You enjoy having it, don't you?"

"Well, yes, but . . . "

"Then let's keep it for a while longer."

She leans onto him, and he raises his arm, glass still in hand, to accommodate her.

"Let's go to your room," she says without looking at him, and he precedes her up the stairs, then ascends to the top bunk of his bed.

"This is so high," she whispers. "It's like I'm high on hope." Her evening gown cascades overboard, a lucky mutiny that's collar-hooked on a bedpost.

When the phone jangles like bugle beads, Andy answers, knowing it has to be Netta.

"I can't," he tells her. Cupping his hand over the mouthpiece, he elaborates. "I can't possibly go to London. But I can phone. I'll see what I can do that way." Then, gravely, he returns the receiver to its cradle, climbs back to Shelley.

At 5 a.m. Shelley sleeps aloft, a plains burial slumber, as Andy slips out and down, toward the study telephone.

On check, Emp's house—which hasn't been moved from the formal dining room—is still, motionless.

With the apprehension that attenuates long-distance, Andy calls London, the Black Letter. "Is that James?" he asks, distinctly enough to be heard across several oceans.

"Who's there?" comes the reply.

"It's me, Andy."

"Well, Andy, I never."

"Listen, I can't speak long. I'm here in Los Angeles."

"That explains things."

"Seriously, James, I need to get in touch with S.U."

"Who?"

"S.U., you know—Street Urchin."

"You mean Sunny! He's branched out now. It's Street Urchin on the Never-Never, or similar; I don't know. He's no longer here, Andy, he's over at the Hangover Gallery. Do you want the number there?"

"That'd be brilliant." Andy is anxious, slipping, as he hears sounds coming from the direction of the dining room.

"Thanks," says Andy, as he writes down the number. "I'm sorry, I'm really in a rush."

"I'm sure you are," laughs James.

Andy crosses cautiously to the dining room as if he were eluding a hulking murderer instead of a small dog. He quickly shuts the French doors, thinking he's effectively encased Emp. Then he returns to the study to make the next phone call.

"Hangover Gallery," he barely hears, as if the speaker means it.

"Can I speak with Sunny, please?"

"Sunny?" the voice sounds hesitant, confused. "Oh, yes. Who is this, please?"

"I'm a friend, calling from Los Angeles."

"I see. A moment."

"Yeah?" says a familiar voice.

"Su-Sunny, it's Andy. We worked together at the Black Letter."

"In Los Angeles, Andy, really. Shame." Sunny cradles the phone between his ear and shoulder while he

runs his hands through his rough boy-bob haircut. It
looks most like the tip of a leonine tail.

"Well, I don't have long . . . "

"To live, y'mean?"

"No, no, listen. I can't speak long, but I need a favor. I need you to track down someone for me." He
quickly explains about Honor, about Simon, about
Sharlott.

"The last one I think I know. She comes in here now
and then, or I see her in the Tate or the Portrait Gallery, sort of stumbling and mumbling about. I think
she gets shooed from there into St. Martin's in the
Field sometimes. But when she comes here, I usually
sit her down with a cup of tea. Harmless, really, without her words. She's like a dead soul, isn't she, there
in her punk-rock jumper. So sad."

"Sunny," Andy interrupts. "Sorry, but I have to
keep this brief. Can I fax you a photo of the other
two?"

"Yeah, but be clear it's for me. I'm just the tea boy,
y'know. I ain't the main geezer here. Say, do you still
have your series of Black Letter t-shirts?"

"What? No, I pitched those long ago." Andy flashes
on Netta's *A* shirt as he hears scratching coming from
the kitchen.

"I have all of mine. My favorites are the ones done
like toys. The blocks on blocks."

"Well, you always were a bit of a Blitz kid, a New
Romantic."

"Still am," replies Sunny. "How'd you know? *I still am.* So fax me the photo and I'll keep my eye out."

"Thanks."

"Well, you know me, the original Nice Chap."

"Yeah," concludes Andy, keeping silent his conviction that nice people ruin lives.

From the unprotected kitchen doorway Emp growls and guards, a black pearl necklace dangling from his purebred mouth like congealed saliva. Emp aligns his jaw with the cut-out ankles of Andy's vaguely elfin slipper socks.

▫▪▪

On her hour away from March Hair, Demona walks down the Fulham Road for Black Letter, where she sits at the counter to have lunch. Spying her from behind, James places his hands over her eyes. "Guess who called not more than twenty minutes ago?"

"James, what are you doing? Who?"

He lifts his hands and answers, "Andy."

"No," says Demona, turning thick-white as cream.

"Truth. From Los Angeles."

"L.A., is it," she says, clicking her nails which she's grown to outlength her fingers. "Give me the number."

"I didn't get it," says James as he waves customers on to seat themselves. "He wanted Sunny's. I doubt that you'll get it from him, though. You know what men are." James laughs cagily.

"Yes, I do, and I also know that you're one, too, if I'm not mistaken." Demona grasps James by the wrist, her nails anchoring like medieval spikes. She leads him to the phone.

After dialing the Hangover Gallery, Demona passes the handset to James. "Now, get it!" she hisses, *it* meaning Andy's phone number.

"Sunny," he says. "James here. Did you happen to get Andy's phone number? He gave me it when he phoned but I've misplaced it."

"There's something here," says Sunny as he examines the fax. He reads out the number on its edge. "There's another number and address here too. Do you want those?" He recites it, not knowing it's Netta's. "But hang on, James," Sunny adds. "This is confidential. Andy is *by necessity* ex-directory."

"Of course," says James, gulping as he hangs up.

■■■

The tensed, taut ankles of Andy are rescued, just in the nick, by Desde who is up with the sun to prepare Emp's breakfast. Fortunately, the lure of grilled liver is greater than that of nervous heels which crack as they go up the carpeted stairs to a warm and occupied room.

■■■

Hours pass and Netta still sits up in bed. She wears just her sleeplessness now, wears it like a bedridden nightgown sprayed the disturbing color of over-the-counter sleeping pills. When she hears the phone she doesn't move at first, but then leans sideways to answer it.

Netta thinks it must be Sunny again, all life and full of assurances that he'll find her mother for her as Andy had requested, that she's not to worry, unaware that his promises are undoing her. For in the foremost corner of her thought broods reason, pointing out that now that her mother's come back to life, she's no longer a haunter but a hater, one who hates her.

However, it's a young woman's voice Netta hears, a voice which identifies itself not as Honor but as Demona, looking for Andy.

"Oh, he's not here," Netta explains, "but I can take a message for him. I'm a friend. My name is Simonetta."

"Simonetta, hello. You mean to say Andy doesn't live with you?"

"Oh, no," she answers, suddenly tired. He lives with his girlfriend who's not really his girlfriend. Do you want the number?"

"Yes, yes I do. I must say this is all sounding painfully familiar. But don't you worry . . . " Demona pauses, attributing Netta's listlessness to Andy. "I have plans to come to L.A., and when I do, we'll take care of him. Oh, yes, we'll get him." Demona rings off before Netta can question, and picks up her scissors which divine her toward a mangy mop of forest-green hair.

□■■

It if weren't that things always happened in the black for him, Sunny would disbelieve his luck for, as he unlocks the gallery Friday morning, who should saunter in but Sharlott, unmistakable in her striped shaggy sweater—archetypal World's End widow's weeds.

Sunny bids her good morning and starts to make her a cup of tea.

"I wanted to ask you about a friend of yours," he calls from where he stands by the kettle. Then he approaches Sharlott with the picture of Simon and Honor.

"I don't know," Sharlott says, squinting from the lux-light off the fax.

"Not him, love, her." He puts his hand on her shoulder.

"Her, well, she's a maid. A spinster night-nurse!" Sharlott laughs.

"Sure she is, love," Sunny says as he plops an extra sugar in her tea.

"She is, for her star. He told me." Her finger rests on Simon's black mouth as if to silence him.

"I often see you in museums," Sunny says, changing strategies. "Are they like prisms for you?"

"Prisms, ha!" says Sharlott as she grasps her tea with fingerless gloves. "Maybe once upon a time. Now they're more like my prisons!"

"I see," says Sunny.

"No you don't."

"But you haven't seen either of these two recently?" he asks, waving the picture.

"I told you," she says, standing now and shuffling her velvet hiking boots. "When she came out of the institution she became a servant. For her hero." She twirls once. "Thanks for the tea."

Sunny wants to ask her to wait but doesn't, especially as he hears the gallery owner coming through the back door.

And Sharlott stops behind Charlotte Street, pulls a playing card from her coat pocket and writes down the numbers she'd seen written on the fax. "Prison," she sighs, to herself.

"Her hero?" Sunny contemplates later that night as his elbows anchor one end of the seesaw bar at Blitz II. If the corkscrew wig he wears suggests his love of T. Rex, the satin jumpsuit clinches it. Sunny looks around the club, this Heroes Night. But all he sees are Bowies and Bryan Ferrys: surely they can't be the heroes Sharlott referred to, although in truth they are the only heroes who really exist.

He orders another drink and follows, for a few feet, a girl he'd seen in W10. But she exaggerates her ignorance of him so, with nowhere else to go, he turns his lonely thoughts to work.

Sunny has to go into the gallery tomorrow, on what is usually his day off, to help set up an exhibit called Heaven's Attic. The show features photography, which he hates, chronicling the goth and gloom years, which he hates even more. The only good part is the t-shirts that were designed for the showing—mock-ups of the Black Letter ones, with the years "1980–?" printed on them.

And then he thinks of the fax, which he'd taped to the backroom wall and stenciled around it in a frame of his own making. MISSING/REWARD, he'd written on its borders, not that it was anything original.

The girl from W10 walks by and asks Sunny to dance, and soon even the pouring rain seems right.

" 'I tried but I could not find a way,' " Sunny sings along. " 'Looking back all I did was look away.' " And W10 covers her weighted, lunar ears.

◻▪▪

At the opening, Sunny is pleased to be an anomaly, an eye-splitting splash of Technicolor in his Stephen Jones hat, in his cadogan kilt. The only touch of gloom is his undershirt, well-hidden beneath layers of clothing. The brogues on his feet, however, are so heavy he has to sit, often, in the back room.

"Tea break again, Sunny?" asks the gallery owner as Sunny hops up, a marionette.

"I ain't one *yet*," he denies, to the Mott the Hoople song, but it's a lie, as untrue as all the lyrics that seem to stick in his mind. Sunny gets another bottle of wine and prepares to go out among the guests. But he stops when he sees a writer from a music paper gazing at the fax-photo.

Sunny wants to tell him that he's not supposed to be back there, that it's not part of the exhibit, but he fears another reprimand from his boss.

"Look!" says the writer to his companion. "It's who's-it, the maid. I'm sure it is. I've played with her cat, Evie, who's all about the house. Oh, she's a plush pillow of a cat, so loving. But her, I can't get the name, but that's her, the American. The quiet one. So quaint, you know, having an American maid."

"Are you sure it's her?" the companion asks.

"I'll have to bring someone from the house to see for sure. But I'm nearly positive."

"She's probably wanted for murder," he continues, in a deeper, more ponderous voice. "I told them there was something not quite right about her. Christ, I think they even found her in a mental hospital." Then he holds out his glass for a refill, nudges his friend on.

Sunny comes forth but says nothing. Another cluster of people has now entered the back room, but it's more than he can control so he shrugs and makes way for the by-now trampled gallery.

"Art is too frail for openings," Sunny says (he thinks) to himself. "It's not meant to be stomped to death by packs of loud, overdressed . . . louts!"

"You're right," says a man seated in the picture window. "But who said this is art?"

" 'This ain't rock and roll, this is geno . . . genuflect!' " Sunny answers, changing the plot as his boss approaches. "Thanks again," he adds, to save himself. "You're so right. Let me know if I can be of any more help."

As Sunny is opening the next morning, the writer returns accompanied by someone with the kind of stacked black hair Sunny hates the most. They head past him for the back, for the fax.

"Hello," the writer calls. "What happened to that piece that was here?"

Horribly, the wall is blank. "Celia!" calls Sunny, to a girl who's arranging the front desk.

"Oh, that," she answers, coming closer. "I think we sold that. Yes, I'm certain we did."

"As a matter of point it's the only thing we did sell," Celia tells Sunny later, in confidence.

▢■■

In the Sloane Square Post Office, Sharlott stands at the far counter. Her cheesecloth Anarchy shirt looms past her torn leather jacket like a half-mast surrender flag. She holds a soft mailing pouch and a small Venetian compact. Were she to open it, she'd discover the mirror is cracked: powdered rouge clots its frozen rivers like lost love.

"I took this from Simon," Sharlott writes, and committing words for her is as laborious as assembling hunt-and-peck ransom notes. "And I think it must be yours. Forgive me."

She fumbles to find a roll of stamps in one of her jacket's compartments. Unhinging the tiny pictures,

she affixes them to the packet which she then drops
into a proud pillar box.

◻▪◻▮

In sequins and terrycloth, in the sleepwear that is
now her constant companion, Netta watches a game
show and suppresses the dread that her mother might
be that writer Andy described. She hears the sliding
sound that means the mail has been slipped through
the hungry box-slot. She walks to the door in carpet
slippers that snag the rug with their cracked plastic
soles.

Netta sees the pillow parcel first; the rest of the mail
lies on top of it. But she slides the other letters aside
in favor of the biggest one and when she takes out the
compact, she opens it.

In the bits of glass there is a woman in a rouge-red
robe. An effigy-cat is her footrest. "Shh," the woman
says and Netta feels hate—she hasn't said anything!
But then it appears the woman in the glass is address-
ing the cat. In her small quarters she's saying, to the
cat, "We're less than no one, less than no one, but for
now, only for now."

Netta slams the mirror compact and tries to cry.

"Nothing worse than trying to cry when you can't,"
says Mario, from just outside the front window.
"Worse than fighting unreality."

"Oh, shut up!" Netta says, refusing to let him in.

"You're as bad as my mother, whichever one she is. Why don't you all just leave me alone?"

With that, the ghost rolls up like a shade. Stronger now that he's freed, Mario heads for Hollywood.

In the dim that's early morning, Andy goes downstairs to the study. He ascertains Emp's absence, then uses his dagger dressing gown to muffle the sound of the typewriter, covering that bay where the keys hit the paper.

He's taken two pieces of paper and one waxy carbon sheet to type identical messages: one for Shelley, one for Netta. "You're so nice," he types. "And that's the problem: nice people ruin lives."

For Netta no longer compels him, and his wanderlust is setting in like root rot. Back in London, he knows, things will be different. He'll find that writer—or the woman in Netta's picture—and he will be set for life.

Andy removes the sheets of paper, leaving the carbon for Shelley. He handwrites to personalize the notes. On Netta's he writes love.

When she gets the note the next day, Netta will say, "Tell a lie." Tell a lie, she'll say, especially to the tiny insecure word, love.

In the rented car at a drive-thru restaurant, Andy sits, waiting for Enmity to open. The only person who'd seen him leave the house was Desde, who softly surveyed his shopping bag and sighed, going off to fetch Emp.

Once the shop opens Andy runs in, shopping bag in hand, full of returns to buy him a ticket out.

"Did you miss us?" ask Antagony and Organdy, all done up as mermaids for a special promotion.

"Like double pneumonia," he wants to answer.

"Did you come to see the Neptune line?" asks Organdy.

"Get hooked," Antagony adds. "Scale new heights. Awful, huh?"

"Actually I just needed to return these things," he says, proffering the linen bondage suit first.

"Quick getaway, eh?" says Antagony. "Jay won't like me taking this back, so I'll do it." And she gives him cash, still cold and stiff in the morning till.

"Headed back to London, I bet," she adds, and in his mysterious carelessness Andy forgets to deny it.

He exits just in time.

Moments later, Demona walks in, on the heels of a conversation with Desde. "She thought I was his sister," Demona muses to herself. "Poor lamb."

When Demona explains to Organdy and Antagony who she's hunting down and why, they're wary at first, uncertain whether to help. But Organdy's mowed down by Demona's cleverness, by what Antagony decrees is her insatiable fiction of desire.

"Or maybe that's just some words I saw on a label," she adds, hanging up a luminous vest. "Anyway," she tells Demona, "he was in a definite flight mode."

"Wherever he is," the stylist vows, her long nails like knitting needles casting off, "I'll get him."

Then Desde runs in, confused, asking the girls for Andy. "I think he has taken the dog," she says, grasping at her breath.

A note had been left on the refrigerator door, Desde explains, spelled out in magnetic letters. "I've got the dog," it read. "He'll never see heaven again."

Demona puts her arm around the shaking housekeeper to assure her. "I'll help you," she says. "Now, were there any clues?"

"There was . . . there was a little plastic train and the words, the words were encircled in track."

They leave for Union Station, where Darren is preparing to affix the tiny dog, who runs small circles in his pet carrier, to the southbound railroad track. "He's here, ladies," Darren cries out when he sees Desde. "I found him." He imagines Shelley covering *him* now, from head to toe in stuck-on showplace ribbons. He seems himself a hero.

As Andy drives to the airport, he finds Mario reflected in the front windshield, clear as an alpine bell.

"Where have you been all my life?" Andy asks, relieved.

"How should I know?" replies Mario, tipping his black beret. "I'm not my own keeper."

Who Is
Sleepwalking
(And Who
Envies Them)?

S kitz is weightlessly confined, a phantom in prison, with time like blue slug-veins on his transparent hands. Time enough he has to thoroughly soul-search, to reflect and peel so carefully he can only reach one destination and conclusion: he will stay exactly as he is. For if people change, he decides, they only change a fiction.

He stands upright in his garage apartment in Highland Park, which is east enough of Hollywood to be idyllic. Spilled seedy bars, nocturnal club life crooks its reapers' scythes just the right distance from his courtyard of smog-sapped eucalyptus trees, from his upstairs room of hardwood dust groundcover and blackout-drapes music. Skitz smooths his variously patterned shirt, lifts it outside his Levi's, and changes to go to work, making deliveries for Caesar's Shadow Pizzas.

Skitz cuts an unusual swath as he carries the hot and

89

damp cardboard boxes in his outstretched arms. He looks like a refracted zombie with his too-blue, gem-plucked eyes as he comes up the sidewalk path, up the driveway, up the stairs, to just outside your pliable front door.

He could care less about you.

Skitz learned long ago that he was in league with the moon, and he has perfected his way of glancing at it. His fate, he knows, is harnessed to the stars, and his conversation is often met by broken sentences that bail and trail off like kinetic bass lines. The silence is the emphasis.

He has spontaneous schizophrenia, selective amnesia; all the latest things, but backward.

And he's happy as he drives, longing only once in a while to live in a Hampstead basement with the paintings all askew, due to subterranean waters.

Today he's alone and loved only by a girl called Chloe, a girl he met and slept with a few times, and then promptly forgot.

◻◼◼

Chloe, despite her abject intentions, is always seen. So pretty is she that stars seem to fall around her face like firefly bulbs on a starlet's mirror.

She likes the morning exclusively because it's nearest to the brighter dream state and she honors the night for one reason only: she met Skitz in it. She was standing, huddled, on the rounded corner outside the Whisky when he passed by.

"Where are you going?" she called, startling herself but not him.

He assessed her slowly as he approached and then whispered loudly in her ear, above the highlighted sounds of the cars that sped along Sunset Boulevard. "Inside you," he answered. "Inside the ghostly spiral that almost cores you."

Because each lived far (she in an older part of distant Orange County), they drove in his car to the summit of Sunset Plaza Drive, to a cleared development site. Surrounded by fairy rings of glistening, empty beer bottles and well above the interchangeably acid-fogged and twilighted city, they held fast. The sex was merely a passion-stabbing for Skitz, but for Chloe, with her childlike fingers in her mouth, it was the love she'd been saving all her strength for.

Chloe has ghosts, micro-incubi, that take over every month just before she gets her period. They stay on for the duration to tighten and flutter through her private moors like Catherine over you-know-who. One day she realizes that maybe fucking during her party-crashed flood might drive the uninvited out, so she tells Skitz her theory, when he's knee-deep in her. She gives away the secret existence of the hide-and-seek incubi.

"Incubi?" he laughs. "I'd sooner succubi myself."

He grins but then, upon evaluation, prefers to kiss not

her source but the delicate shadow-slits airbrushed like bracelets at her wrists.

"You make me think of my joke," Chloe tells him suddenly. "It goes, 'Do Dracula's victims go down for the Count?' I guess not." She withdraws her arms from him, matches them over her heart as if she were topless. By now she has perfected her trait of spouting inappropriate things to Skitz during his elaborate pinnacle of sex; by now, too, she is about to lose him.

After he disappears, her lack of him is consumptive so Chloe develops a thing for the pop star she previously had no idea Skitz took after. Chloe becomes a backward fan: she joins featureless, impersonal fan clubs, puts up paper poster-ghosts for mirrors, and removes CD liners to cut into wallet snapshots. She only does this to keep Skitz alive for herself, caring little for the pop star except to feel sorry and somewhat embarrassed for the look of pain he often wears as if it were the reward for his efforts. It's hard, too, for Chloe to feign obsession with the abstract, since she believes such an act is always about nothingness.

"I love you," she'll say, primarily to Skitz but through his musical medium. She'll say it, as if ritual made a difference, each night in the visionless, tooclose air that comes just before sleep. Chloe sends him boomerang, carrier-pigeon thoughts that huddle and edge toward extinction while she drifts off, numbly tired from her full day's work at a decrepit theme park. Her calico and gingham costume is placed on a white wicker chest at her feet, and the outfit is a warm-blooded contrast to the marble girl it daily drapes, like leaded weights.

One morning she wheels the stick-boned tea trolley right up next to her bed and then crawls back beneath the covers. Instead of mixing cream into coffee, she pours powdered activator into bleach, a concoction for lightening hair. Her gold tresses she'll turn into straw, a kind of reverse alchemy.

Once morning is overcome, time starts to drag. Indistinguishable hours, days and darks, tend to blur and blend as they find her leaning on the counter of the food concession where she works. She pauses often enough to stroke her hands through her stiff hair and then brush off the dust that lingers like dry ice at the hems of her skirts.

The time doesn't move because it's all the same, Chloe is certain. She wishes she could embrace the idea of death's relief the way some of her friends do, especially the handful who've just drained their spiked sarsaparillas and scurried off in the direction of the park's ghost town, where they'll easily see spirits the presenters have laboriously failed to deliver.

But Chloe snubs death, knows that her grief would only be intensified in the afterlife: more futile—fathomless, even.

As Skitz reclines in the laundromat, the idea of Chloe does not even edge on the outermost fringes of his thoughts. He thinks instead about his clothes, which he loves almost without exception. He stares at the porthole window on each dryer and has to suppress a laconic cheer each time a particular favorite lunges into view. It's as if he's watching a sporting event, not a lazily churning dry sea. Occasionally his work uniform with its black and white goalie stripes will appear, only to be trounced by a punk-rock dog pile of black and clanking metal.

Skitz reaches into the front pocket of the jeans he's wearing and retrieves his pay envelope. He unfolds it, pausing to admire his name displayed in the wax-paper window. He opens the packet and finds a flyer attached to his paycheck.

"Calling all employees!" it reads. "March 15 marks the second annual Caesar's Shadow night at Gingham Ghost Town. Sign up now for special low-price admission. There's no topping this!" Penciled in at the bottom is a note from Skitz's night manager: "Et tu, homey?" Skitz laughs as the dryer stops turning and the clothes drop flat like disappointment.

He will stop at the drugstore on his way home, to cash his check. He prefers this, having a bank that also serves ice cream. Then Skitz will go home and change into his prison stripes, to head for work.

As Skitz enters the mini-mall pizzeria, he sees his manager Kevin jostling and jousting with one of the other delivery boys. "I swear to you, I left it in the mailbox," the boy says. "No way was I going to go up to that door. There's probably a moat full of hungry black widows lurking just beneath that trapdoor porch. Tarantulas, even. Or land-mine piranhas."

"But the mailbox?" laughs Kevin. "No way can that be. How could the pizza even fit?"

"I folded it," says the boy, Ephraim, as he leans over in laughter.

"What?" asks Skitz. "What's going on?"

"Oh, nothing, man," says Kevin. "Ephraim's been making some creative deliveries. Don't let him give you any ideas."

"I'm off," Ephraim announces as he hugs his black corduroy car coat around his body. His barber-pole legs protrude like licorice sticks.

"Aren't you gonna change first?" Skitz asks.

"It's too late for him to change," says Kevin, ringing up No Sale. "Anyway, I can hardly say *you're* a credit to the uniform."

"Fuck off," says Skitz quietly, watching Kevin help himself to some cash. "But Kevin, man, what was Ephraim so destroyed about when I came in?"

"It was nothing. He's just weirded out about that place on Isabel, the one that he thinks is spook-ked. You know the one I mean?"

"That worm-eaten monstrosity that's the color of pond scum?"

"That's it. He left the pizza in the drive, man. Bastard. Next time I'm sending you."

"I ain't afraid of no ghosts," says Skitz, as he does a little dance. "In fact, they're usually afraid of me. But wait, do you think that's why they ordered from us, because of, like, Caesar's ghost?"

"It can't be because of the pizza," Kevin says. "Anyway, I'll be back in a while. If anyone asks, say I'm at the El Sereno store because we ran out of . . . anchovies."

"But no one ever orders anchovies."

"You'll think of something. Who's working the register tonight?"

"That new chick."

"Ofelia. If you have to fuck her, wait for me."

"You're sick, man."

"I know. Dam-maged." He waves as he goes out the back door to his motor bike.

When Ofelia arrives, the first thing Skitz notices are her eyes, green like the sweaty color of oft-handled money.

"It's okay working here," he tells her. "None of us are serious, and you're just in time for a wild night at Gingham Ghost Town."

Ofelia nods softly, her thoughts hours back with her boyfriend.

"But the cooks are stupid," Skitz continues, motioning toward the sequestered back. "You have to remind them to breathe."

The blue strands in Skitz's hair look like tinsel, Ofelia decides; they're Christmas tree icicles.

⬜■▨

Kevin, Ephraim, and Skitz walk three astride in bad-guy black toward the entrance to Gingham Ghost

Town. Once inside, Skitz joins the line at the covered wagon food stand where Chloe works.

When he sees her, he's puzzled at first, confused by the harvest of hair that sprouts like stalks from out of her white eyelet bonnet. He stares at her elastic neckline, at her gathered waist, remembering the lush circles and folds that lie beneath her hester-prim costume. But to recall this is a stretch: at present, Chloe's body is a mere conjecture of shapes beneath all the material.

"Leave the counter," Skitz whispers and Chloe tilts her head down to hear him. "Come down those wooden steps and be with me. We'll take the cavern train ride. My tongue can be a stalagmite in your darkened throat; my fingers will drag your river, and that mock-musty scent will cling all around us . . . "

"I can't," Chloe stops him. "I'm working."

"When you get off then, or on your break."

"I don't get a break, 'cause I came in late." She had been disturbed all night by ghosts that made her room change shape: her headboard sailed, respectively, north south west east, and then pointed down like a runaway raft through a course that was bordered vertical, octagon, pentangle, obelisk . . . "But I might be able to leave a few minutes early."

Chloe meets Skitz at the far limit of the park, in another theme area. She watches him standing beneath the neon, rocking-horse moon that watches over the Depression Dance Hall. Chloe observes him as he animatedly gestures to a girl he's with and then becomes subdued when he turns to what's probably her boyfriend.

"Hi," Skitz says when he sees Chloe. He turns to the girl he's with. "Ofelia, this is . . . "

"Chloe." She holds out her gloved hand. A velvet satchel droops from her wrist.

Ofelia smiles. "And I'd like you to meet . . . " But Ofelia's boyfriend has gone back into the ballroom.

"I like your necklace," Chloe tells Ofelia, fingering her dainty crucifix. The writhing body is a delicate filigree on silver planks.

"Thank you," Ofelia says, "but I better go."

When the park begins to close, Skitz and Chloe arrange to caravan back to her home. She instructs Skitz to hide by the shrubs that decorate the garage, which angles thumblike from Chloe's parents' L-shaped ranch house.

"There's some brick tiles that trim the front hedge," she tells him, "so be careful not to trip on them."

"Nothing stops a Caesar's delivery boy," he laughs. "Not rain nor hail nor spooky flapping sheets, nor . . . " He feels in his breast pocket. "Nor condoms."

"Wait for me to turn out the front porch light," she concludes, opening the door of Skitz's black Starling for him. "Then I'll go through the house to let you in the garage window. You'll have to crawl over the washer and dryer so, um, crawl quietly."

"I'll be like a velvet mouse."

Chloe leads the way home and she feels the draw:

her car is a tugboat and Skitz, an undertow, a notorious riptide of never-rest.

Deep in the wicker forest of Chloe's room, Skitz looks around and tries to decipher the shadows and contours of her wall posters. He turns to find her already quietly in bed, and feels like a favored toy as he slides up against her.

"I left my ribbon on," he explains, tugging on the ascot which hangs loosely from his neck. "Stuffed animals always seem to wear something, even in bed."

Chloe puts her arm around his neck and kisses him. "I missed you so much that I know this can't be real."

Then she pulls back. "It's weird," she explains. "When you haven't had sex for a while, the whole idea becomes kind of as remote as the moon. The blue moon, even."

"The moon misses the sky when it's away, you know," Skitz replies. "And that's how I missed you."

Inside her he is a full, late-harvest moon, eclipsing, she hopes, the subterranean spirits that tide in her. They drown in shadow, she prays. A natural disaster: No Survivors.

At the first notice of light, Skitz turns toward Chloe and stirs her. "Should I go?" he asks. "What about your parents?"

"It's okay," she yawns. "They go to work really early. They won't come in here." She cuddles up to him but he moves away, gets out of bed to examine her posters and pictures of his pop star.

"Is this why you like me?" he asks, pointing to one as if it is a visual aid.

"Come on, Skitz," she answers, sitting up to feel the first sharpness of cramps. "I liked you before him, before I even knew about him." Her forehead hurts, resounds like a dribbled basketball.

"What's wrong with you?" he asks. "You look like you're cross-eyed."

Chloe feels the approach of dry tears but manages to say, "I'm fine."

"I better get going, anyway."

"Skitz," she calls, as though he were far away. "Will you be with me again?"

"I'd follow you anywhere," he tells her, adjusting his belt. "To the ends of the earth."

He turns as he walks toward her bedroom door. "That is, until people started to talk. Can I just go out the front?"

After he's gone Chloe gets the heating pad from her chest of drawers. Curled and drawn, she clings to it while cradling the spindly, awkward handset of her elaborate French telephone.

"Timpany," she says. "Timp, are you sitting down?"

"It doesn't matter," comes the reply. "I don't have very far to fall."

"Guess who came over last night," Chloe says and the other girl settles in, several dozen cul-de-sac loops away.

Later Chloe is still on the phone, calling in sick to

work only to find out it is her day off. She passes the day in bed, never leaves her room. All the soap operas she watches seem to tell the story of her and Skitz, but a shade off-kilter. It is their poorly-recepted selves that waver and don't match up a quarter-inch around each actor's body.

Chloe watches speechlessly, her platinum hair pinned up of its own will against the headboard. She doesn't talk back to the t.v. as she twists in search of a comfortable position. Beneath her nightgown she is sweaty and musty — her perfume and powder combine to make a kind of exotic nightshade in her body's crevices.

And then she starts to mourn, feeling sad for all the time before, when she and Skitz were apart. This she feels entirely: the residual death of things.

"How do you see me?" she'd asked him the night before.

"In fits and stars," he'd answered, on the spot.

◻◼◼

When Skitz looks at Ofelia's softly shaded eyes what he sees are the tattooed, jagged tears falling from her boyfriend's granite face.

"What's with your boyfriend?" he asks her, his cree-pered feet pushing against the plywood counter.

"Who, Corazon?"

"Unless you have another one."

Ofelia laughs an airy laugh, one that would be sarcastic from anyone but her. "What do you mean?"

"I mean, does he ever talk or does he just stare?"

"He talks," she replies, still standing at the counter although she could sit, kick back. "But he only speaks to tell me he loves me." Her pale eyes are like high beams.

"And what about the tatts on his face? Are they really for homicides?"

"They're not tears. They're halves of hearts. He puts them when he breaks up with a girl and the girl tries to kill herself or someone else over him."

"What if she's successful?"

"Then he'd make a whole heart."

"I don't get it." Skitz says.

"Well, he's with me now and we're happy. That's what matters. So no more galaxy of hearts. No more broken tears. Just love, everglades of love."

"Smoke a lot of angel dust?"

"No, no," says Ofelia. "I never do drugs. Drugs flood the heart."

"This is beginning to make me sick," says Skitz, looking at the phone. "Come on, phone, ring."

"Your girlfriend?"

"Girlfriend, what," he says. "I don't go in for that 'walks in the park' stuff."

"You were with a girl last night, I saw you. And she loves you. I can tell by the way she looks at you."

"Her? No way. No. Last night I came home—alone, I might add—and I put out the lights, put on some music, and rolled around on the floor while listening to it."

"That's love, too," says Ofelia. "She probably did the same as you."

"She didn't," Skitz says nervously. "That I can guarantee." But his extended lie now tugs full-force at his insides and he runs toward the back of the shop, for the bathroom.

A few nights later Ofelia sits reading a photoromance book while Kevin and Ephraim mess around, taking turns imitating her soft-accented voice when calls come in, and then writing down orders in her perfumed hand.

"It's fine with me," she tells them, "whatever you guys do."

The boys laugh, pushing each other harder.

"Ofelia, you should come to one of my shows," Kevin tells her. "I'll even write a song for you. Call it 'The Story of O.' "

For Kevin, Ofelia has perfected the art of indifference.

"You'd like the band," adds Ephraim. "Kevin wears velvet dresses — and daggers and crosses."

"Why would I like that?"

" 'Cause you like religion?" tries Kevin, desperate.

The phone rings and Kevin grabs for it. "Caesar's Shadow," he says, in Ofelia's liquid tones. He listens and his face suddenly goes stage-white. "Yeah, sure," he answers, "we can do that." And then he replaces the receiver gently as if it were something he cared about.

"That was the house on Isabel," he says, looking off. "They want to order fourteen pizzas for tomorrow night, to be delivered."

"I'm not . . . " starts Ephraim.

"You're right you're not. Skitz is. Do you know what they'd pay in that house for someone with black and blue hair? Have you ever heard of white slavery?"

"But he ain't white," Ephraim says.

"Except for the lies he tells," laughs Kevin.

"Are you leaving?"

"Yeah, after I make sure Skitz is scheduled to work tomorrow. Then I'm gone. To Susan's. Got to catch up on my sleepwalking."

"That's Kevin's word for sex: sleepwalking," Ephraim tells Ofelia, who fails to look up from her reading.

"Why can't you or Kevin go to the house tomorrow?"

"Ofelia, it's haunted! Plus it stinks. It smells like sulphur soup."

"No wonder they like our pizza."

◻◼◻◼

As Skitz's answering machine stiletto-steps on to record Kevin's message, Skitz stops in his doorway to hear it.

"Make sure you come in to work tomorrow. I have a new tape I want you to hear."

Skitz, reluctantly habitual about work, grimaces. The job is one thing, but he'd rather crawl across glass than have to listen to and then critique Kevin's band.

He turns out the overhead light and heads for Fullerton, to meet Chloe.

Ofelia leaves work at 3 p.m., a short time after Kevin has gone. She stops at a charity clothing warehouse just off San Fernando Road, with the intention of buying some junk jewelry—big-beaded ropes to offset her timid crucifix. As she walks through one of the rooms that's cluttered with see-through curtains and stained, hopelessly frilly aprons, she spies Kevin in an eastern alcove, enmeshed in modeling a lace camisole.

She quickens her pace and smiles to herself. "Some girlfriend," she thinks. "Sleepwalking, no way. His only passion is standing up, to be looked at."

☐■■

Skitz, off-track and very lost, enters a grocery-mall bookstore in Placentia. "I need directions," he tells the clerk, only to be hailed by Susan, Kevin's unmanageable girlfriend, who brandishes a Bible-sized copy of *London Fields*.

"What are you doing out here?" Susan asks, as if seeing Skitz were fantastic.

"I'm trying to get to Fullerton," he answers.

"To the school? That's where I'm going! Do you want to have a drink first?"

"Well, ah . . . " Skitz is reluctant to say no to Susan, who attained some glory as a fictional diarist/epistler. There is always the chance he might say something she would use. "Well, I could, but really I was on my way to the Shambolic."

"The Shambolic? As in the nineteen eighty-four-era Social Distortion Shambolic? You and Kevin: time-warp city."

"Same time, different warp."

"Same city, different . . . no, that doesn't work. Never mind. What about that drink?"

Skitz sits a safe distance from Susan in the echo-noisy, empty bar of the Red Onion. Waiters angrily ignore them as they move quickly, preparing for the soon-to-be-packed happy hour.

"I wouldn't think this would be the kind of place you would like," Skitz says, with the vague annoyance that he's keeping Chloe waiting.

"I don't like it. I hate it. It's just that a long time ago, when Kevin and I were here . . . "

"Kevin was here?"

" . . . there was this guy. He came up to me and took my hand. He was dressed the way Kevin does now but didn't have the nerve or the insight to, then. He looked, you know, like a poet-priest, but not perfect, not like it was a costume. He looked like he went out that way in daylight, even. To work! Like he lived in ruffled tuxedo shirts, kilts, and jewels. You know.

But anyway the guy took my hand. 'That guy you're with,' he said. 'He's in love with you. I can tell by the way he looks at you.' But at this time, Kevin and I were barely getting along. 'No way,' I said. 'You're wrong.' He insisted he was right, but then when he asked me to dance I politely declined."

Susan stops to sip her beer through a straw.

"And then he went straight to Kevin," she continues, "and supposedly told him the same story, with the same line. I don't know, that's what Kevin said, anyway. But I wonder what happened to that guy."

"Maybe he joined Social Distortion."

Susan just sighs. "You don't get it at all, do you? Mixing metaphors like they were these cheap drinks. What's wrong with you?" She picks up her crescent-shaped handbag and starts to leave. "And stop staring at my purse. I'm not going to pay for this."

Skitz stands on the anemic pavement gazing up at the Shambolic's crest: a withered shamrock that's more a four-leafed, four-legged Celtic cross. When the neon is on, it coats the bar's soon-to-be denizens in a slimy shade of bad-luck green.

A cartoon-sized clock is hung over the bar and it bears the Shambolic's motto. "Deep Enough 4 Drunk" whirls counter-clockwise around its face on which all the numbers are fours.

In the Shambolic, it seems, it's always unhappy hour.

Social Distortion repeats on the jukebox. The music is loud enough to mask the sound of the trains as they lunge past the bar's back door, hurling grey and black gravel like magic dust.

When Skitz finds Chloe she's propped up against a gothic column, her cheeks a paler shade of teal. He buys more drinks and then corrals her toward a booth where she sits but won't look back at him.

"What's wrong?" he asks. "What did I do?"

"I don't know," she says. "You go, you come back, and everything's misshapen."

"What?"

"Then, too, when we're not together, all I can think of is that time we were apart, and it makes me feel horrible. All those months when you forgot all about me or never knew about me." She lifts her drink, a zombie.

"Chloe, you don't give me much credit. It's always been hard for me. No bed of roses, for sure. A bed of thorns is more like it. Even growing up: I'd sit through closing prayers wishing I could keep my eyes shut against the other boys who'd all be showing each other the tips of the knives and blades they had, the prelude to the after-school fight. I'd be mapping out the quickest and least populated route home so I could avoid the whole mess. I couldn't fight! And then when I decided to move out because I was sick of sharing a bedroom with my horrible sister, I had to get a job.

"I thought you liked your job."

"Oh, it's all right, but it's hard work sometimes."

"Mine is, too. But I'm sorry for you."

"I'm okay. I mean, I like, you know, my clothes and

my music. My hair. My place is okay. But it's just that sometimes I have these dreams that I have a basement flat in London, in Hampstead, and all the pictures on the walls hang crooked due to subterranean waters. Only all the colors I see are bright yet they're soft, and it's the polar opposite of my present."

"I understand," Chloe says, upending her shiny-with-residue glass. "I sympathize."

"No you don't," Skitz answers. "That's the whole problem with you, Chloe. You have no sympathy. You're so sad that all you can manage is empathy."

He leaves Chloe, dwarfed and almost swallowed by the forest-green tuck-and-roll booth. She pulls at a piece of vinyl tape that masks a tear in the seat and then removes it to reveal a slug-trail of adhesive gum, black and prolific.

She feels with her feet for her gym bag that has her work costume tucked inside, and then pays the tab. She drives to Gingham Ghost Town.

In her concession stand, the alcohol weighs heavily in Chloe, and it rattles and riles her internal demons. Her lower insides twist like heartache and the weight of her forehead prompts her to lean, to rest her elbows on the counter, her face in her cupped hands.

Chloe frees her right hand to take down a customer's order. She fails to stand straight and forgets to say thank-you. By the time her shift is over, she has been fired—the customer was an employee, a relative of the park's owner, even.

The reason for her termination was formally cited as Leaning.

The next afternoon Skitz phones Ofelia. He doesn't want to come into work and Ofelia, remembering the haunted house scheme, urges him not to.

But at 4:30 he appears, looking strewn and exhausted.

"I thought you weren't coming in," Ofelia says.

"Yeah, well. Is Kevin here?"

"He will be. I don't like to say anything, but . . . " Ofelia pauses. "But I think Kevin's really weird. I think I hate him."

"Nah, Kevin's all right," Skitz defends. "I kind of feel sorry for him, even. He's like the last of a dying breed. Him and his fingerless gloves and fungi-black nail polish. He's clinging to extinction. I mean, at least I have my icon, my role model. At least I have company." He thinks of his hair, uses a palm-sized comb to push some of it down, against the grain.

Ofelia isn't sure what Skitz means, but she smiles anyway.

When Kevin comes in, Skitz starts to worry about the tape he was supposed to hear. That Kevin fails to even mention his band should have been Skitz's first clue that something was askew.

■■■

Chloe sits at a filigree-metal and marble-topped table in Watson's Soda Fountain, a tangent of the City of Orange's bracelet-like traffic circle. She fills out a job application while gazing out the windows at the uncharacteristic afternoon fog. It is a weather condition of her childhood, she remembers, now long gone and muted like innocence.

As she's inking in the blank for her sex, the fountain's doors fly open like automatic wings. Chloe looks and looks again — without averting her steady gaze. She feels disbelief physically (it feels like a thrill) as she stares up at the shape and visage of the pop star she mock-idolizes and Skitz emulates.

Up close the star looks toylike and unreal, and all Chloe can think is "Taxidermy!"

She starts to approach him as he orders a vanilla shake. No wonder he's alone, she thinks. It's only the bravest sort of person who would stand by a walking doll of a human.

◻■■

Skitz carries the last two of fourteen pizzas destined for Isabel Street to the delivery van. Even the cooks come out to watch him leave. Ofelia privately crosses herself.

"You guys are crazy," Skitz calls from the driver's window. "It's just a house in Cypress Park. You know, a place where people live."

"And where the dead are alive," murmurs Kevin. "Alive and thirsty for new black-and-blue blood."

⬛

At the TV Motel in Anaheim, Chloe slowly undresses for the pop star. He doesn't talk much, she notices, but oh, can he kiss. He kisses like he's pulling her feet first to the other side of life.

⬛

Skitz parks the van in the soft dirt of a side street, right up next to a derelict ice cream truck. "Cuidado Ninos," admonishes its side, but when Skitz peers in, it appears someone's living in there.

He takes a stack of pizzas, plus about an inch of flyers, promoting Kevin's band, that are customarily delivered with each order instead of napkins.

There are two broken stairways that lead to the enormous, hushingly dark Greek Revival–style house. It looms like a silent master overseeing the tiny and flat houses that lie at its feet, across the dropped lash of Isabel Street.

Only one light is visible. It comes from behind the fan-shaped window above the doorway. As Skitz walks on the rotund lawn (scaling, for fun, the low green moguls), he sees a cat. He puts down his parcels to pet it and makes out the animal's name on her heart-shaped collar.

"Perdido, eh?" he says softly, scratching the cat's chin. Perdido leans until she falls onto Skitz's feet and then she stands up to lead him to the porch. He pushes the pulsingly-lit doorbell and then looks up at the attic tower, at the encased gaslight. How could he have mocked this wonderful house? Its soft green color is reminiscent of algae-strewn jelly, it's true, but from his vantage point on the porch, the city beneath him is a black pond by moonlight, teeming and glowing with lush and distance-thrilling microorganisms.

Skitz gets the feeling that there's someone to his right and then to his left, hide-and-seeking around the huge pillars and then flapping up behind the skirt-curtain of the fanned window. When he looks at the tops of the pillars, he sees that key pieces, big chunks, are missing. How can they support the heavy clap-board overhang?

◻◼◻◼

When the pop star finally kisses her sex, Chloe feels as if all her insides are shaken loose, and that they float out. She is lit within by uninhibited blackness, her empty stairwell resonant with sounds of joy.

It's then that the gargoyle incubi take wing and fly on tiny griffins to land in an entryway in Cypress Park.

The people Skitz sees are miniature, the size and color of American Beauty rosebuds.

"Sorry to take so long," they tell Skitz in unison. "We were in the attic."

"Perdido, no," says the man, Beauregard. And Lei-la, the woman, pushes the door shut with both her arms, closing it behind Skitz but in front of Perdido.

Skitz puts the boxes of pizza down on a jagged marble table, recalling that he's long considered the veined white surface to be the only sure magnet for ghosts. He prays for the appearance of some life-sized ones. As he faints to the floor, Kevin's flyers flap and fall like paper manta rays.

Leila and Beauregard lasso Skitz's thumbs with embroidery thread, to climb up on him.

"I don't know that he's worth living in, dear," Leila says, surveying the mat whites of his eyes.

"Maybe not," says Beauregard, setting up a camp cot in the forestry of Skitz's hair. Beau looks down, spies the treasure map depicted on Kevin's flyers. "Leila, come," he calls. "Here's a boy that might be more our speed."

Leila walks over and hand-claps her agreement. "Still, let's have our fun with this one first," she says, proffering a tiny needle.

◻▮◾

When morning comes, Ofelia and Ephraim open the pizza shop. Neither Skitz nor the delivery van have returned.

"He'll be gone for a poet's eternity," Ephraim shrugs, saddened.

But Ofelia phones Corazon. "I'm not sure how we'll find his girlfriend," she says quietly. "But maybe my want can draw her to me.

"Yes, I love you, too," she says, ringing off as Kevin comes in.

"Don't blame me," he says. "I was only playing a joke. I didn't really think he wouldn't come back!"

On her lunch hour, on her first day at work in the soda fountain, Chloe is in the bathroom stall, writing graffiti.

"I Slept With What's-His-Name," she scrawls, in case anyone's deft enough to believe in the liberation theology of the right fuck.

When her training is done, she drives north for Caesar's Shadow.

Ofelia embraces Chloe as she enters the store. "My boyfriend is waiting for us," Ofelia explains. "We have to hurry—they have Skitz!"

Corazon is silent as he drives the girls up the steep and circular roads leading to Isabel Street. In the late afternoon light the house is verdant and cool, an edifice shadow for Perdido to play in. The cat stops stalking a moth in favor of approaching the people. She rubs their legs and then follows them to the doorway and across the threshold.

They find Skitz where he's been sleeping, discarded in a closet. His black and white t-shirt has been crewel-stitched to his skin to read, in blue hair-thread:

"For What Are Ghosts But Earth-Pricked Angels?"

Chloe, for one, knows it's a trick; there are no angels.

Corazon and Chloe walk the sleeping Skitz to the car while Ofelia calls for Perdido. In the front seat the cat bats at her crucifix, only to tire and then sleep curled in her lap the rest of the ride to Skitz's apartment.

Later, when Skitz awakens, he pleads with Chloe to never leave him, to stay always by his side. She embraces her positive reply, a resounding, unanswered happy ending.

◻◼

A
Stay-In
Story

*U*pon careful second thought, Jinx no longer
wants to know the story of her life. Who
cares? She, for one, is tired of running around looking, for all the world, as if she had the sky to catch.

Especially now, as it's falling in globule-sized eggs,
pelting her roof like a poltergeist would, as if her tiny
home were yet another outcast, just one more guilty
pariah.

Jinx places a prefab log in the featureless mouth of
her fireplace and returns to the sofa, to sit comfortably
on a blanket that temporarily covers the snarling glitter upholstery. She sips at her hot chocolate and then
pats the place beside her, an invocation to Jude, her
grey, ocelot-spotted cat.

The cat is still new to her; she just recently liberated
him from a cat show, where he'd rubbed his eyes raw
against his metal-flaked display cage. During the judg-
ing of the Cat Most Likely to Succeed, Jinx slipped

away from her friends (pleading her extreme legion of allergies) to rescue the pint-sized animal.

It hadn't been a moment too soon: Jude was scheduled to be judged next, as Most Unusual, because his tail culminated in a Latin Cross, at eerie and perfect right angles. But instead Jinx slid the pet into the inside breast pocket of her felt coat. He's been right up close to her heart ever since.

That is, of course, except for tonight, when he's being mock-reticent and flirtatious, elaborately rebuffing her invitation. With the crash of thunder that accompanies the opening credits of *The Hand That Rocked the Coffin*, a horror film Jinx has rented, Jude is off, out the whisker-width opening left in the sliding glass door.

Jinx just sighs, refusing to run after him, and she settles in to watch the film.

The story opens in Bucharest, in a village square, where young people cling to stone lions. It cuts quickly to Berlin and shows a nightclub deejay (one of the youths from the square) using his fingers to find records to play, knowing them by touch more than by title. A white mouse cowers in a corner; a black cat pounces. Then the deejay has disappeared from his console: only his hand remains, spinning and respinning the jump-start disc.

"Well, Jude, you're missing it," Jinx announces, more clearly than she usually speaks. She has a habit of talking to others as if she were talking to herself.

Jinx stops the film and gets up, to muss her hair.

"Little girl with a crooked part, has no one to love her," she'd been teased all through childhood. As she looks at her outlined self now, however, in the sliding glass, she's pleased and happy with her locks that are an exotic shade of brown, with hints of paprika that shine when infrequent sunlight hits them.

Most often, though, her hair is straw-mud-colored, because Jinx avoids the sun. The sun is a white plague that makes her sneeze and wheeze, accentuating all the starbursts of dust that linger no matter how much she cleans. She has taken up swimming to escape the air, to become a kind of chlorine Ophelia, loath to surface.

Tonight, however, it's okay. But it'd be better if Jude would come back.

As she starts the movie again, a scratching sound comes from the door. Most likely it heralds the triumphant return of her cat, who, curiously, can always fit on the way out, but needs to have the door opened to come in. He must swell with pride when he's outdoors, Jinx concludes, he must puff himself up. She unfolds herself to rise, glancing at the t.v. screen where a bouquet of choking baby's breath claws at a coffin, mirroring the sight just beneath, where fingerbones tear at the other, quilted side.

Jinx walks (like somebody already gone) to the door—to widen it. A falconer's gloved hand curves from outside the glass to slide it along its trolley. Before him, Jude scurries in.

"Look what the cat let in," the boy says by way of

introduction, and in soft and accented tones. He is shadowy and of even height, has center-parted dark hair and suit-of-armor eyes. From his ears hang pairs of metal shellwork earrings, and he wears delicately tooled leather trousers. But his main feature, apart from his sullied and cumbersome wings, is his bass player's primary pout.

"Have you something to drink?" he asks.

"Hot cocoa," Jinx replies, staring.

"That was it, I think," says the boy, looking at the crib note written on his now uncovered wrist. "Rococo with marshmallows."

"No, cocoa," Jinx corrects as he follows her to the kitchen. His heavy wings trail behind him like a bridal train, enticing Jude, as Jinx flaps a packet of instant cocoa at him as if it's a shingle hanging in a storm.

The boy faintly scowls his reply. "Might I have a mug of tea instead?"

So Jinx boils water and soon hands him a milk tea the color and texture of raw silk. He's now seated on her bar stool and when Jinx looks at him, she feels like the ice in the bottom of a drained drink. She realizes in that moment that He Knows Things.

"Are you psychic?" she asks.

"You are," he answers. "You're perceptive to the point of being psychic."

"Are you a ghost?"

"I'm an angel," he laughs. "Except on Sundays, when I get to be a vampire. On Sundays I work on my night morale. On Sundays I dress up in ecstatic black."

"I always wear black," Jinx answers. "Everybody around me nowadays looks like a calliope of colors, but deep down I know there's always something to wear black for. People make fun of me for that but I don't care. And it's my lack of caring that reverberates and lasts."

"And your Reason that broods the most," concludes the angel, who is Swiss.

Jude rinses her hands beneath the tap and then wipes them on the hem of her black t-shirt, which shows an iron-on punk-rock group accompanied by the written legend *I liked them before you did.*

The angel slides off his bar stool to give Jinx his empty mug, and she notices that he isn't very tall, he's barely her height. His eyes, mostly lashes, are delicate, refracting and shattering the overhead fluorescent light. Only his eyebrows are disconcerting: they look like streaks of artificial cake frosting, like they should spell out some ominous warning.

"I'd like to call you Befana," announces the boy. "A witch who rides on the epiphany."

"Okay," says Jinx, who leads the angel into the front room. "What should I call you?"

"Claude," he says, and Jinx hears "Clod" so has to suppress a sneeze.

A growling emanates from the television, where Jinx's snaggle-toothed v.c.r. has chewed up the videotape. "Damn!" she shouts. "What do I do now?"

"Why distress?" Claude asks. "It makes your hair

fall out in gulps. You'll end up like me, all downcast wings."

"Don't your wings work?"

"They do. They're just so tedious when I'm at rest." He settles them around and at his sides where he sits on the sofa. With his long fingers he lifts a snowflake doily to expose a cobweb of dust.

"Why'd you do that?" Jinx cries, her face now red as nail polish. Her eyes scratch and crawl in their jagged sockets.

"I didn't do anything that wasn't already here," the angel defends, hurt.

"When I feel like this," says Jinx, "I don't even want to live. I can only look forward to the unique end of time, because I don't want to kill myself."

"That is the universal wish not to live."

"You're right. I don't want to live when I can't breathe. It's like suffocating by degrees."

Claude stands and approaches the distraught girl, and Jude positions to make a play for his matted feathers.

"Stay away!" Jinx commands Claude. "I'm sure your ratty wings aren't helping my circumstance." But the angel edges nearer. "You, too, Jude, always locating me with that pointing tail!"

"Original thinkers," encants the angel, "and poison-drinkers, come rally 'round us." He enfolds Jinx, uses his fingers to part her hair, and then kisses her swollen mouth with alpine rain. Jinx tears off her clothes in a fit and with the angel she has sex which is like the funnest pillow fight of her slumber-party youth, in the days before her allergies took hold.

He leaves her wrapped in a clear cocoon, a protective lattice-lace shell to precede and follow her like a guiding guardian shadow.

In the morning, too, there's a ring around Jude's tail, making it a less obscure distance-signal antenna, a stone-cutting Celtic cross.

High
on
Hope

*f*lying home I use my ragged fingernails to pock
     the fullpage skin; it's the minor key I write in
     I gain a day but I don't want it, wish I could
bomb-boomerang it 'cos it's a day apart from you

I've been cheated out of a moon but you know the
moon can't be female; it's the careless creviceless point
of some hidden man

who feels nothing but the flowers of punishment

I'm driven out at night while it's still light and will
have to remember

The best clubs he says play one song, nay one *riff* all
note I mean I'll night—all night. I love the bass for its
understanding but he doesn't need that

I wish I were a dole queen, that my painted foot-
prints, my murder-outline feet could always lead instead of my stupid head

I thought being apart would be like hero-worship
but it's not: not even. It's always feeling off, out of

125

speed and playing a record you love although it sticks and blacktop skips

But when you're there bystanders, strangers, suddenly appear as messengers, penciled into the scene to offer bodings and tidings and then strobe dreadlocked off, sigh-of-relief chorus

In Ladbroke Grove a man with an Ethiopian dagger says he'll pray for me, in Battersea he'll pray for me. But in Kings Cross I change, lost again. Not really: I change in Euston and dutifully walk a few blocks up.

I went around the corners of your body and now live only for your scent, the only air I can lushly breathe

White bone candles in heavy-handed Notre Dame and Allan Kardec's boasting bust—these comprise the legs of a triangle and their blood gushes at my feet as I straddle loving you, your kisses the most tangible memories

If ever you're not there and if ever I run out of time, don't come to my grave I'll surely pull you on with me

If I can't find you, he says, I'll uplift you, see you writing in and out of consciousness, love you in spite of it live in such

a heaven

Like Goth Never Happened

Part 1: A Sea

*a*ll the while I shouldn't have been with Aidan; I should have been off along the ruins, consorting with the various crusty black lesions of musicians who cover London like so many umbrellas.

Or maybe like my friend Netta I should have gone to South America where tornadoes dog-ear and spit-curl the other way around, instead of coming to a place where I'm told people wear telling rings on the opposite extremities.

But how was I to know? I chose a place where after all I was fluently bilingual: that is, I could write both $ and £.

"Olive, I pity the man who becomes your boyfriend," my cousin Nell told me right before I left, but I pity *her* with her dopey boyfriend who eats penny-candy off the ground like it'd be bad luck to leave it there. The kind of guy who mumbles "Oh, no! Oh, no!" just under his breath whenever you talk to him but when you ask "What?" he'll look down and say "Oh, nothing, nothing." The kind of guy who deserves not to be on the guest list but on the double-price list. The kind of guy who . . .

Did I mention that I still love him?

Every night at 10 p.m. I ride the Circle Line trains while I say the rosary. The stations—not the stations, sorry, but the mysteries—are so much more dramatic underground. You see, even the most abstract faith in God is a better bet than love.

Netta was right, though, about going to South America. She's the kind of girl who doesn't belong on the ground.

But as for me, I need more of a full-time miracle that could prevent me from investing with a soul everything I see; to keep me from viewing sexual fidelity as high-concept.

As I sit in Mansion House station I know what I have to do: the writing's on the hallway walls and on the slashed seats in front of me. It's scratched out like an idea over my head. I walk through the tunnels in a full-length transparent dress but my hands are full—a candelabra in one, and an aiming, diving, divining knife (antique of cross, I mean of *course*). I know what I have to do and in this moment of decision, my past falls away from me like the cellophane sea rolling backward.

Part 2: Guy-Wire

I wonder now, does lying require a degree of sophistication?

"Nah," I can hear my morbid cousin Death Nell saying. "A simple certificate will do."

I tried to call Death Nell yesterday, from a festival booth where a phone company was offering free long-distance calls. I punched in the digits on the keypad, making the sign of the cross there I'm sure. Then I bleated my needs before being mercilessly cut off. I don't know if it was Nell I reached; the connection was kind of waterlogged, but the echoes embracing my words were encouraging whispers from a spot-light-blind crowd.

It's not life, though, but all love that's a stage.

I stumbled out of the humid, tented booth (wet hay stuck to my dm's like bad news). I bought another lager.

I wanted to ask D-Nell to pray for me. Her and Only Her prayers had worked fail-safe for me in the past, but now with all this bitterness and acrimony between us, what am I to do? It probably wasn't she I spoke to, anyway—it was probably Monte, true object of my disaffection.

I put the poignant, pretty knife back into my hippie bag and smooth my dress. I change trains at Baker Street.

I read the note I've prepared for Aidan. (Happy Aidan, but not for long.) Aidan, who tried to waylay me from the doom and gloom I so love, which fits me like gabardine gloves. Aidan, who tried to convince me *E* was for ecstasy, never knowing that *E* was the letter eternally missing from my soul's composite report card.

I move through Baker Street passing the buffet station while I recite the note from memory. I try to recall which mystery I should be at. I think the joyful mysteries would be best for Aidan: they could smother, enshroud, and strangle him in his hammock-smug happiness.

Strangers jostle me but I walk on, the jousting knife jangling up against a lipstick tube. "You'll know," I whisper. "One day you'll know how much I loved you. And the knowledge will follow you around and haunt you. So then you'll have to become a goth, a gloom-rocker. You'll have to, to disguise the embarrassment of being followed everywhere by this cloud, this mangy sheet on a guy wire, forever two full steps behind and above you."

I breathe. "And your feet will grow buckled, ending in Pinocchio-points."

My vein-colored Metropolitan Line train comes and I get on it. Someone has left a jacket draped atop the parallel seats and it looks like a big cat there, like prize game.

After I kill him I hope he'll oblige me by staying dead.

The Virgin Mary is visiting her cousin Elizabeth by the time I near Harrow-on-the-Hill. Some little goblin is jumping around pistonlike in old Tin Lizzie's womb.

I see the crackerjack-toy ticket inspector reflected in one of the mirrors of my Indian bag. He gets bigger, more distorted before he asks me if he can see my ticket. He could, of course, if I weren't a fare-dodger.

Part 3: The Ticket Inspector

He leads me, his forefinger looped through my bracelet chain. The Ticket Inspector is a thin-faced, fair-maned man wearing a dark, stable uniform that features a knee-length mod coat. I protest all the way in my broadest American, but he's heard it all before.

We travel the train two stops back to Preston Road, where we disembark and he takes me to a sicky-green room, a kind of holding cell. But I wonder: why am I by myself? When will I get my hippie-bag back?

These thoughts run around in my head like the Circle Line itself, and like my rosary which I've knotted at my forehead to make an exotic headband, for luck. I know I must have some kind of rights. But I know too that I've lost my passport, lost it soon after I arrived, right after changing thousands of dollars into small clutches of *avoirdupois*.

Still, I know what people do in these situations, and it'll be a cinch for me. I sit down on the wan ticking-cot and reach between my legs. I unsnap my white lace bodystocking at its crotch and part the two halves of floral-cloud material. I knead my white gown up to my waist, and I wait.

Soon I'll ask for some paper. Didn't that work for Oscar Wilde?

I wish I had a mirror, or at least my purse where I could redux like a Busby Berkeley nymphet.

I know my hair could be better. It's the color now of wilted bed-lettuce, and curly lettuce where it protrudes beyond bread crusts. I take the rosary off and hang it from the prison bars at the foot of the bunk.

My hair might not be at its best but my body, as always, is a sure shot. Perfectly proportioned and soft, it's a beauty-queen prom-dream beneath this damsel-poet gauze-guise.

I know some people think of their body as a temple; well, I think of mine as a flophouse, open to all comers.

I hear the sound of heavy-soled shoes, shoes that keep out the cold. Their throbbing matches mine but mine is kid-glove warm and custom-fit inside.

I start without him, my hearing straining over the descending sound like raw silk stocking over marbled thighs.

It's then I think of Death Nell, of when I first saw her.

My family lived in central California, inferiorly north of Nell's Los Angeles. Her mom was visiting mine and I was characteristically indifferent to the newcomers, quietly hating anyone who caused me to leave my playroom (a screened-in service porch). But

I left my grown-up dolls to meet Nell and her older brother, and we went to the schoolyard.

Nell ignored me and played only, intently and deeply, with her brother. To get her attention and gain admittance I went to the swingset and climbed on a narrow slit-swing. Straddling it, I swang sideways, to show how it was done.

I must have crashed forehead-first into a steel pole. I only remember (by being repeatedly told) Nell and her brother carting me home on a borrowed bicycle.

If you trust someone with your unconscious, I mean, what's left?

I think now of how that swing seat felt, its slimy width, how the braided chains holding the swing sounded, clanging. I jump when I hear my jailor's key twisting in the peephole lock, a perfect fit.

"Not here," he says, looking past me. When I stand, the hem of my dress falls back to the floor.

He leads me to the empty signal cabin and I use my breath and wrist to polish the faded flat buttons on his coat. I pull up my dress again and he pushes me against some rough cushions, taken from the trains I think. He's in me then, this prince, his scepter knighting and beheading me.

A train (our Grendel) passes beneath but the Ticket Inspector just keeps at it, pummeling and thundering on until his release, a jeweled snail trail in my cunt and running tentacle-like down my thigh.

"There, then," he says. "I'll just go and get your things."

I want to tell him I don't want my things, now or ever—I only want him. But then that's the waylaid way I keep getting into trouble.

Part 4: Back in Bayswater

It was Aidan I was concerned with, after all, before I was, uh, sidetracked.

He has this kind of smile that's candles in daylight, redundantly brilliant. Plus as I sad, *said* before, he wears this prescient happiness, a forward-mask.

There's a message from him waiting (like roses) for me on my phone machine when I get back to Bayswater where I live and dwell. The playback is all "did I want to meet him the nest, *next* day in Regent's Park" and not much else, a soft tunnel-flower.

When he sweats in bed from the drugs it's like crying-jag loss. It makes me so wordlessly sad; he's asleep and I'm not.

I had my hair in a patterned scarf the night we met, or else we never would have.

But I'll sleep now until we see each other in the park and walk parallel asphalt lines on a fenced-in green island jutted by ghost-exhausting cars.

It'll be fine then; it'll be like goth never happened.

Often in my life I've suffered from the voodoo of being too sure, but where Aidan's concerned my feelings flip-flop like sandals at the seashore. I'm buried deep, then I'm free but slapped. Flagellant grains sting the two-white backs of my legs. See what I mean?

I'd like to think he's laced with corruption, the way drinks are spiked, but in fact he's probably as innocent as syrupy church-punk, *punch*.

The mistake he made was in gratuitously breaking, *breaking* my heart and that's why it behooves me to kill him one day, to end him off, the anti-goth.

I remember the directions he'd given me to this place, how he'd written in this sexy backhand slant, so like the way he fucks.

I keep compulsively straightening my sitting tomb, *room*, when I realize the rosary's missing. I left it in the green cell where I never asked for paper. I left it and I'll have to get it back.

Checking the mirror I see a pimple on my too-round face, near my drop-equator mouth. I put a felt-tip marker to the spot and now I have a beauty mole, an angel's love bite. It must have been a cherub to leave a mark that minute!

Then I put on my pep squad jacket. It's bundle-bunting for my happy day ahead.

At the station my lips intake the vermilion train. You see, I can't stop trying to think about my past, any past.

In Regent's Park I meet Aidan; his headset necklace is delicate earmuffs. One day, I know, he won't remove them to hear me speak—he'll just nod in tempo.

Whether it's early or late the London sky is keeping mum, but Aidan's arm around me is gift-wrapping.

He is a Catholic child carrying his sissy satchel to school. His drawn steamed-milk expressionless face. His eyes the jewels the hungry crow was after.

No, he should never have gratuitously broken my heart.

Over a closing tea in a sticky cafe he teases me about the skeletons in my closet (for my having been a goth). He says I'll give my first-born a death rattle.

To prove I'm more, I accompany him to his choice, a rave, that night. The sweat turns my beauty mark into a long black, red-cored tooth. No one notices, though; they just keep moving, smiling and kissing in the slosh harbor.

When it's over I can't sleep with him. His mind is as transmitted as the little stereo. We share a taxi back to my flat and I close the lid on him in the black car. He is blissful, matterless.

At home I lick the magnet worry-doll I've made representative of him. I prop it up against my alarm-stereo. I tune into gloomy music to siphon from him his gift of insomnia.

I get in my bed naked and think of how I only do two things with men: get drunk or have sex with them, for that's the realm of the hopelessly shy — the passionate acts.

Part 5: While I'm Still Warm

I wake up sick from the wondering that invades sleep even — I can't lose the feeling that I'm one puzzle piece short of epiphany. My stomach's in knots and crosses: what, exactly, did I need Death Nell to pray for me about? What part of my child-mind (my only mind) did she collect and save—rare steely marbles from my chalk-circle skull?

If we're all born at an indeterminate age we keep all our lives, how could she walk away with mine? Like what has become of the twin taken from us when we're relieved of our soul?

And, this is really one long rant, isn't it, one moan, 200 pages of solitude. It's a sticking record riddled with pothole graves, especially when I'm thinking about Nell.

I know, anyway, I'm doomed to end up alone and ruined like Jean Rhys, destroyed by real and imagined sorrows.

I look around my room and I hate the minutiae, the larvae of my life.

Maybe it's something my murder plot can cure. I was going to kill someone, Aidan, and then absorb him. My shameless, shambolic, shambled love, then, would alternately drag and sound the cracked-clay depths of my wishing well.

And now I hear my neighbor Camden stirring, closing cupboard doors and filling the aluminum tea kettle with equally metallic tap water. I sleep with Camden, of course, and I feel like doing so now.

I get out of bed and put on my thick-with-fluffy-growth chenille robe, its corn-rows pointing the direction of dissent, *descent*. I drop it suddenly, in one fell stroke, to be revealed like a sculpture. I go to the wardrobe and retrieve instead my 1950s quilted shorty, to offer Camden the kind of weightlessness most men never know.

A silk accordion-bleated, *pleated* scarf I tie at my wrist to use as a sweatband.

Camden is alone this Sunday morning, I think, make sure, as I listen at the hallway door. I wriggle my mary-jane dance slippers as I tap on the door.

When he opens the door he sees me, a morning paper between my perfect teeth.

He's tall, in plaid tattered pajamas, and wears last night's drunk like a shrunken wool sweater. But he can be persuaded out of it, like out of his clothes, into a lie-down and out of a hangover. He chews my ear and then my clit like indie-pop gum and the music he listens to, all boyish bop and no bite. He waits a while before going down so by the time he does, I've already come, several years before the masticate.

I wander, *wonder*, eye our morning shadows soul-kissing in silhouette until Camden falls back and asleep, surrender by collapse.

I don't love him any more than I love myself. And when the phone rings I'm sure it's his girlfriend so I answer, telling her we're reading the paper together. No lie, just my own version of the truth. I wake Camden by swatting him with the folded paper and return to my own room to brew tea, to brood.

I think the reason my memory is so lack, *lax* is that I never told anybody anything that happened. I never repeated it so it never got lodged and logged in the gimcrack attic of the mind that is supposed to account for reminiscence.

I had a therapist once who suggested a barnstorming style of hypnosis to make a bridge to my past. Never mind, I knew. If it involved a barn, I'd be off in the hayloft, *un*alone. Maybe now, though, in telling myself these things, in my self-consolation, memories will peek through, sheet corners of lost letters, phonetic photo albums.

And how about you, are you really such a welcome repository for all this psychodrama?

I try to recall my phantom playroom, how the gritty screens made a kind of permanent twilight that always attends the call to come home, the end of play.

Last night, too, I forgot to do my circle rosary. It slipped my mind like left luggage.

Remember, I went from Aidan to the surfeit, the *sure fit* of sleep.

There's a tap on my door and I can tell by the sound of manicured nails that it's Camden. He's come to return the newspaper and some magazines. Because, after he fucks me up one side and down the other, I'm planning to look for a job.

Part 6: Dance to the Radio!

A look at the calendar reveals it's still this year, and that's close enough to be the date of my job interview.

I travel to Camden Town (I know, I know—but this time I keep my hands to myself) to go to this fashion firm called Clothes for Liars. I enter the big, newish building, loathing my day-old salad-bar hair, reminding myself that's what happens when you go through green. I should have stopped at red.

The assistants cease whatever they're doing when I walk in. They all look like store window marionettes.

The head designer interviews me, but I don't catch her name. She questions my accent and the legality of my working. I explain that I'm English but my boyfriend is American and, being a natural mimic, I can't help myself.

Then she asks me about my career plans. I tell her I see the career ladder as more like a stringy suspension bridge with gremlins starboard and port jumping up and down to startle me. They're dressed in rickrack–hemmed cutoffs and carry patch purses that hang from sticks to look like lollipops. I hold onto the ropes so as not to fall down for the count, down into the muddy Mississippi, into shallow old Owl Creek.

The woman smiles and hires me as a messenger, I guess 'cos I got the Knowledge.

When I walk out, one of the puppets, called Aubrey, pulls me aside.

"Be careful with Her," he cautions. "You need special shoes to be around Her."

"Huh?" I say.

"To walk on eggshells."

I leave and head for a cafe, but first a phone, to call Aidan.

"How are you, all right," he says (he always says that). I tell him about my job and he's happy, if abstract. But he can't meet for coffee because he has to go to work, to his job as a signalman.

So I go to a pub instead and have a gin and tonic like a good girl. Halfway down, I re-evaluate my plans.

(1) I'm missing my rosary.

(2) I'm missing Death Nell.

(3) Nell needs to be told about her boyfriend, that he's not who she thinks he is.

(4) What to do about Aidan?

It's the last thought that I stick with, the one that stays too close like the cocktail napkin (now sheer from glass-sweat) stays at the base of my drink, pinafore-like.

It bothers me that Aidan doesn't care about my life but then, I couldn't care less about his. It's as if, apart, our details are irrelevant because, I guess, we should always be together.

I love him, I do, I love him so much heaven-and-hell has no meaning.

And he might love me in return; I don't know, he wastes so much time on what I call the magnet responses. You know: you say "I miss you." He says "I miss you, too." You say, 'I want you." He says blah-blah.

But watch this: it never works with "I love you."

Never mind, anyway. I'd rather be missed than loved. So I guess I'm the luckiest girl in the world.

Once I've finished my drink I leave the pub. It's started to hail at weird angles, as if someone from behind is throwing not his voice but ice from my abandoned glass.

I should go up to Preston Road, to find the Ticket Inspector, but instead I'm transfixed by a couple kissing. How I yearn to prop up the walls that way!

I go to a music exchange in Camden Town, looking for sex.

The only suspect (indeed, the only person in the shop) is behind the counter. He's okay, vauntingly goth. The only color on his person is set into his floral denim jacket.

He looks at me with annoyance and I decide he's the best kind of angel—the one with an evil stripe.

I undo the top mock pearl buttons of my gold cashmere sweater. The guys looks, at first, but then looks away.

"Lock the door," I command. "A madman is chasing me."

He doesn't look.

"He has a gun."

Still nothing.

"And a rottweiler."

The guy comes slowly out from behind the counter. He's a little overweight, but I like that.

I follow him to the back, to the dust-sparkled stockroom.

"We're not alone," he says.

"So?"

There's a mottled sofa in what could be a kind of lunchroom, and I back the guy called Sonic—Sonic Bloom—onto it. Then I sit on his hands.

A radio plays Joy Division. Ian Curtis, patron saint of all goths, martyred advance guard. He sounds happy.

"I love your fingers," I tell Sonic. "I love them most of all 'cos they're inside me."

Suddenly he's a tower of strength. It's off with his leggings, off with my lace panties, all that. In the end it's a fair exchange: I laid him and he inlaid me with his Johnny-jump-up, with his slippery-as-mercury primordial ooze.

I kiss him long before starting to leave through the back entrance but he pulls me back and I close my eyes.

"I love you," he says and my lids roll up like one freshly-zombied.

I leave post-haste and remember to cross that place off my shopping list.

Hours later I still haven't been able to reach Aidan so I go home, to sleep. I lie in the bed zig-zag, like Beverly Hills crosswalks and side-angle-side sex. And I sleep nude, save for my crucifix which sign-posts contrary directions in the valley of the shadow of my breasts.

I dream of the living: Nell with the portland stone skin. Guess that means I'll hear from the dead. At 2:30

a.m. I am awakened by a solitary sweat, heart pounding and pondering as to why Nell was so much more adept at love than I. She could fuck anyone and make it come true.

In my youth Nell's image stuck to me like a humid ghost, all up against me, balled up between my legs like a rayon nightgown on hot, sleep-started nights. But if she knew of her impact on me, she didn't show it.

When I was coming up in this life, surfacing from the drowning pond of my childhood, Nell was the revenging angel I grasped for, receiving only voluptuous palmfuls of air. She was older, prettier, the most remote member of the family (and therefore she had to be the wisest). Plus she was leaving the Los Angeles suburb my family had now joined hers in, and moving to Hollywood.

I chiseled off the heels of my plastic glitter play-mules in efforts to imitate her workless-horse mary-janes.

Today Nell lives in Los Angeles with the boyfriend named, she thinks, Mario, but I know him to be his nice twin, Monte. You see, long ago Mario bilocated the way saints and schizos do, handy in scrapes and rather like *The Palm Beach Story*. It's Monte I adore and I reason that once Nell knows the truth—that she's with the wrong one—she'll step aside and let me at him.

Before he split, Mario (showing his Monte side) used to pick me up from high school once in a while.

In his blue Nova he'd give me such tender rides home before he went on to join Nell.

A good way to explain the difference between Mario and Monte is this: Mario used to play basketball. Monte never would. Monte was the one when Mario was in the air, having hang-time.

Although some claim he overdosed, the real Mario was last seen in a convertible heading for LAX, squinting into the sun and the passenger side sun-visor mirror. He was checking his looks and then paying for them like they were excess baggage. Mario got the looks and Monte got the soul. (You didn't think it was even, did you? No, twin-splitting is like drumstick-wishing: one gets the luck, and the other, the pity.)

I get out of bed and turn on the radio. I feel a burning rash and know I must have been given a disease by that guy in Camden, the one who said he loved me.

Part 7: Real Life (And Worse)

On the night of the glorious mysteries, someone is ascending. I wish it were me but instead it's close enough, it's the Ticket Inspector. I show him my sex, where I'd stowed my ticket, and he pulls it out, to punch it with his incisors. He tells me how he's kept my rosary for me and fondled the smooth prell-pearls in lieu of my nipples and other things.

The next morning I go to work, where I've become

quite friendly with Aubrey. He's telling me about this book he's reading called *5,000 Miles and You Still Don't Matter.*

"It's a way of getting over people, just leaping over them as if they were hurdles. It's most useful for long-distance romances and the tedious jet lag suffered by those who go through them. You should read it, Olive. It might help you get past your American boyfriend."

For some reason Aubrey's method-act lecture has brought me near tears. "I'm American too," I blurt and then catch myself from falling further. "Lapsed American, I mean. Please don't tell anyone. I could lose this job."

"Your secret is locked in the treasure chest of my heart."

"Where have I heard that before? But, about what you were saying about that book. See, I have this theory that there's no such thing as unrequited love. It's patently impossible. The world revolves around the collision made by love—and wills—meeting. There'd be too much of a void, a vacuum, a lack of gravity if one loved and the other didn't. It'd be too much like sex: in-out. I also think that when you're loved by someone really brilliant it's that much more intense because it functions on so many different levels."

"Yeah, but who around here is loved?"

"Good point."

Suddenly I wonder why I ever had this pre-ambition

of London. Why didn't I just stay near Monte and tough it out? What was the nature of *our* collision that had body-slammed me this far—far from home and running puny errands for Her?

Late that afternoon I see Aidan again. I'm so happy my face is starred with tears. We have a picnic in some woods and fuck standing up inside a hollow tree trunk.

I've always been pretty sure that Aidan didn't love me, but it wasn't until now that I realized by how much.

"I was stupid to fall for your lines," I tell him.

"They weren't lines," he replies.

"They are now." I gather up my skirt the way I would the picnic blanket, and I run.

◻▪◻▪

At work I'm pulling stray straggles of thread from bolts of fabric using the technique my mother always warned me against. When a thread finally breaks off at the root, I twirl it and twirl it and then let it fall to form the initial that, as luck or legend has it, belongs to the person who loves me. Over and over it lands to make snaky, spindly *S*'s, uncrossed dollar signs. Once in a while it forms a backward, dunce's white-washed fence *S* but I don't know what it's trying to prove.

Like a desperate game of dice it never falls the way I want it. And baby needs a new pair of shoes.

Instead it just keeps floating and falling, looking like a funnel cloud. And looking like a water spout.

I have one letter from Aidan which I keep beneath my pillow like a lost tooth, festering and fostering the falsest sort of fairyland hope. Sometimes the characters of the words he wrote rise like linotype and leave impressions on my sullen, swollen cheeks.

Hurriedly I replace the bolt of material I'd been unraveling, sensing that someone is coming. But it was a false alarm.

I think of the story I'm telling you as a gaudy cocoon, a gauze-cast mummy in which I might wrap myself to heal and protect. I cast a glance at the patterns Her has set out: all hoods and anoraks, the garments of farewell, the clothes Aidan wears too well.

I feel about me the illegible memory of goth, which I once held around me, warmly and complacently. I loved its place in rock's rich tapestry and how it was my life, which I wore until Aidan arrived to snag and irreversibly one-way ladder the weave.

Before him, I'd loved only pale dark boys who were as tall as they'd be buried, and the mournful, leaden music that was a hapless, sleepless wake, really, for the death of punk (or so Monte told me).

But my memories are defiled now and I am unloved. Aidan will have to pay for what he's done. I collect my distilled venom like pollen. He has defied my emotional law of gravity, of love's supply and demand. He has torn me apart from myself.

Part 8: Pull Yourself to Pieces

I try hard to betray emotion as Camden manipu-
lates me in the back seat of a cab. A specimen-slide of
smeary glass separates the driver from us, the couple.
Camden, of course, has a girlfriend who's not-really-
his-girlfriend when he wants to fuck me. My silk panties are so new-worm wet he mistakes them for me so
I guide his fingers inside, all the while stone-faced.
Soon he's 1-2-3 fingers neat in a residued tumbler.

We reach our destination and I wish he could leave
his hand there and pull me along as if I were on a lead.
But instead we get out and head for a brick corridor
where, standing behind me, he grabs my breasts like
he's a harness and pulls me back into him. And he
comes, all raw-omeletty down his baggy jeans.

But then, who cares? It's just another time-waster.
I'm here alone on the ship-wreaked, ship-wrecked island whose revelers are going down dancing into a
quenchless drench.

Aidan loved me to the letter, all right, provided it
was the letter *E*, the inward vowel. I tell him, tell his
shadow at all times, "You're just nobody from
nowhere."

As for those who are afraid of their own shadow,
well, they're not one of us, one of I, in-crowd of one.
I'm not. It's not my shadow I'm afraid of, or my shadow that has me looking over my shoulder. It's my
ghost.

This night becomes my first irrevocably and finally

apart from Aidan and I pull his cummy sheet between my thighs (although he's never slept in my bed). And I writhe.

Then I fall into a flat dreamless sleep and I wake up covered in bruises, brush-with-death strokes the color of the hair on the head of a poignant guy I'd seen somewhere the day previous. I'd been drawn to him like the vein lines on a child's carbon slate. It's sickening, really, and it makes me aware I'll never be free.

For a moment or two I halfway believe that everything's okay until on comes that creepy realization, adjusting to abrupt light, that something's wrong, something's missing. It's then I remember what it is: Aidan doesn't love me.

And that's the way I prepare to face the day, conjuring emptiness the way some people partake of a fortifying breakfast.

I get ready for work wondering what's the glue (besides sex) that keeps any two people together? And what's the serif-point (curled fetal and in on itself) of these some 50,000 words (average five characters each) in search of a match-point plot?

Is it just the taunt of making up these dense pages, making them appear as grey matter, as grey areas, as hard to read as tombstone headlines?

I walk to my train station, my rosary clanking in my purse like devalued slug currency. I ride the tail-wagging-dog's body train to Camden station and then lumber, leaden, to work. Aubrey's already in, making coffee with another guy, Darwin, who always carries his annoying beeper.

"Oh, Olive," says Aubrey. "Her wants you to take a parcel to Velvetty Records. Apparently one of their pop stars wants to wear something of ours on t.v."

"Right now?"

" 'Course not. It's early. Relax. Do you want some coffee?"

"Tea, please." (I know this takes longer.)

"Bad night?"

"They're all bad."

"Christ." Aubrey slogs the teabag around in my teddy-bear mug.

"I figured it out, you know," I tell him. "It's like when you're with someone and however much you might try and deny it, you keep knowing deep down that something's missing. And it's true—something is. It's the piece, the part the bastard will use to hurt you."

"I thought you only cared about the sex," Darwin butts in.

"I do, Darwin," I say. I figure that if I offend him, he'll retreat. "Most often I do it standing up so it won't last. But it backfires, you know. Lasts longer, defies gravity."

I must have lost my touch because Darwin just stands there, looking blank.

Then suddenly Her storms in, like a worried thought on a cloudless brow. We all make busy.

I have this horrid notion that Darwin wants to go

along with me to Velvetty Records. At home, in California, people have beepers for only one reason: they deal drugs. So maybe someone at the record company has an itch that only Darwin can pinpoint.

Sure enough, he drives me there in the tinny van.

"Were you as popular in Los Angeles?" he asks me, looking to and fro as if he were the windshield wiper.

I realize Aubrey must have sung about my nationality. "I was the loneliest girl in L.A."

"And now you're the loveliest in London."

Yucchh. "It's only because I made a conscious choice to snub my past and move, stuck up, ahead. Today my only conflict is the friction of some guy's single-pronged magnet sucking and puling at my fragile filings."

When Darwin smiles he reveals a big gap in his Easter Island teeth.

"Are we there yet?" I ask, stirring in the palm of the van's bucket seat.

It's weird; telling Darwin this personal information, coming clean to someone I hate, makes it take on a meaning a sympathetic ear could never have drawn.

"*Simpatico* is the only word that can't be translated that I still understand the meaning of," I tell him suddenly.

"Angst," he says. "Zeitgeist."

"I hate the letter Z."

"Zed."

"Hate that one worse. Anyway, D," I venture (and

it doesn't take much for me to venture), "what's with the beeper? What's it for?"

"My pager?"

"That." I point, trying for once not to be vulgar.

"It's so that I don't miss my calling."

"As what?"

"I'm a deejay. You didn't think I do just this, did you?"

"Do what?" I was never really sure what Darwin did, other than hang around looking sulky.

"Besides this job I work clubs and raves. I'm also a part-time night watchman at Kensal Rise Cemetery."

"What's that like?"

"It's good. I take my boombox and my tapes — and my beeper — and I go to the cabin. If it's slow, I sleep."

"Is it ever fast?"

"The music is."

I pick up a tape from the black shoebox that's on the van's floorboard. "Key of E," it says — techno and house music.

"You see, Olive?" Darwin says while parking the van. "There's more to me than you ever dreamed."

"I don't dream much and when I do, it's to have nightmares." I slam the van's door.

"Come up with me sometime," he calls, all Maybe West. "I'll take you up to my berth."

We walk into the record company's reception office, Darwin trailing me like a sidekick.

As we approach the lavish, embarrassing reception desk that's crowned with ridiculous gold-plated discs and portraits of Velvetty's presumably tortured artists looking dull and tone-deaf, my eyes vaseline-pan the scene. They vacillate and then freeze. For there behind glass rests the ghost of my soul, my beloved Death Nell! And behind her, almost as an afterthought lighting her, is Monte.

Shakily, holding onto Darwin, I deliver my swaddled bundle to the receptionist. I stumble out, my legs moving spiderlike as if they were inside of me. In the van I bury my face against the dashboard.

"Do you know who that band was?" I ask Darwin without picking up my head.

"Which?"

"Witch?"

"Sorry?"

"In the photo, the guy and the girl."

"You probably mean the Match Girls."

I hate pop music now and do my best to ignore it, believing the credo that music prevents you from thinking for yourself. I explain this to Darwin.

"That's why you should come up to house music," he insists. "It never claims any other purpose than to move your feet and free your mind."

We drive past a phone box which has a ladder propped up against it—its dowel-steps warping and woofing across the stickered portrait glass and peeling wood. I feel like screwing in the phone box, gleaning the inherent bad luck. Any partner would do—anyone except Darwin. Then his beeper begins its mad-dog mewling. He pulls curbside for the phone box, but I abstain in the car.

I ask Darwin to drop me off in the Kilburn High Road. I move along its filthy sidewalk, slinking and sinking into depression. I look up at the naughty-lace–trimmed windows that tint the storefront flats which crowd the road like unyielding pedestrians. I search the windows for the reflections, the bordered faces of Nell and Monte.

My blood freezes and speeds like time-lapsed photos of freeway lights, the way they become a stream. It courses when it should coarse and then I see a guy I keep seeing. He's studying his filigreed wings, *rings* with jewel-blue eyes that look askance wistfully. He walks like night falls and when he smiles it's to himself and not to me.

I turn back to go home, to sleep 'cos that's all I can afford as comfort. Once in bed I turn and jolt on the fine layer of sand that passes for bedding.

Why am I doing this, scribbling now in my near sleep? Is there a kind of truth here that keeps cropping up like that bad penny? And truth *would* be a penny and not a bottle cap—bottle caps have better edges.

This is so stupid. I pick up the book Aubrey has imposed upon me—the one about loved ones and 5,000 miles. For some reason it makes me think of the Bible, and I've always preferred the rosary.

I slam the book like it's a worn hymnal come loose from its spine and I cross the room to retrieve another, *Ambition* by Julie Burchill. I sit up in my night chair to read and eventually fall asleep with it. I cross my legs over it.

I wanted to dream that I was Susan Street's daughter, the way most people imagine they're Marilyn Monroe's. I wanted to have a ruthless goal worth fucking toward instead of just the derailment, defusing of my past. But there's nothing I want to be when I grow up.

I stay in London like a foolish parish ghost, thinking I'll gain my prominence as if by glee. I survive on a g-string budget spending my currency of incoherence and pretending I'm anything but Miss America. Even when it's obvious I should leave I make my excuses and stay.

You may read with disinterest this arch triumph at best, a nudge-nudge read-read. It's awful.

Actually, it's a jugular-vein attempt to give Aidan a dose of his own poison, a baby bottle of black milk that will taint him and free me. Shame Monte, trash Nell. Make only me look good.

All I want when I grow up is to defy gravity, its down-dragging reflection.

Part 9: Carbon Dating

I think it's morning when I awaken disappointed. Instead it's the hollow heart of night and I can only hope Camden's alone.

As I head toward his room, I pull on my crucifix as if it were a lavatory chain.

Camden's up, all right—he's up like a candle-rod chandelier, watching a corn-fed video nasty. I stand in front of the screen and the picture filters through me onto my white Victorian nightshirt with its spoilt chokehold collar. Soon I'm miming what the pump-and-juju puppet show behind me is doing. My toby collar is all that's left once Camden's ripped the shirt clean away.

He exhales big, and then asks me how I've been.

"Nothing going on but the rent boys."

He laughs but keeps looking at the ceiling. I dismount and freeze-frame the video. "I don't know, Camden," I say from the corner of his room. "But I think I need to talk to someone."

"Fire away."

"I'm obsessed by this idea of a soul mate. I can't stop looking for mine."

"That's normal, I think." His cold voice has a carved marble reverb.

"I know I've met him or her. But I don't know which one it is. They're all reluctantly vying: Aidan, Monte, Netta, Nell."

"Me?"

"You I just keep around for a footrest."

"Cunt."

"I never said I wasn't."

"I love you," he laughs. "You and your rancid luck."

"You don't know the half of it," I tell him, and explain about the encounter at Velvetty Records.

"It's just a coincidence," he says, turning on his side and elbowing up.

"Coincidence is fate's cruel tease. Oh, I don't know. Maybe I just can't articulate how much I want to be the one that got away."

"You must be, to someone."

"I'm not. They all don't care. They're all relieved." For some reason I think of Sonic. "I'm nothing if not gone."

"Parasite lost."

"Fuck off."

"You first. But Olive, maybe you have sex too much. Not that I'm complaining."

"Sex is the insatiable sound track of my dreams. It's replaced religion, it's replaced goth."

"One time you told me desire was a death sentence."

"Oh, I stopped writing. The paper was like soft butter. What I scratched out there would never last."

"Oh, no," he laughs. And I hate to hear those two words.

"I thought you'd meant something different. I thought you meant 'sentence' as in 'Life Plus 40.' "

"Oh, that too. I mean, the arrogance of someone imprisoning you beyond your years. Now that's religion."

"I have a story to tell you," I continue, climbing in bed alongside Camden, who rolls his eyes. 'No, listen. I was in a club, right, on two separate occasions. Each time I stood in the same spot, and each time I met a different guy who I went home with. Now, one had approached me from the left, the other from the right. When I was in the club, I mean. Shouldn't the one from the left be the devil and the one from the right an angel of God?"

"That's crap."

"Hang on. Except for the fact that I'm on the other side of the world, on the wrong side of the blanket. So it should be reversed." I know Camden is too bored to point out that isn't really, technically, the other side of the world.

"Well," he yawns. "What do you think?"

"The one from the right didn't have real sex with me—but he did send me a pair of earrings that incidentally the guy from the left said had attracted him to me. So maybe they should just cut out the middleman and fuck each other."

Camden locks my neck in his elbow grip. "I have the solution for you. Write a ghost story and put all these characters in it. The one that prevails, that's your soulmate, who's S/M-nagging you."

Satisfied, I'm an S now against his body. "Mm," he says. "MMm."

Back in my own room, the dawn is soon a girl-slit at my pained horizon, a landscape with a rebirth I endeavor to avoid. But I pick at my notebook like it's a persistent scab, to test Camden's theorem, to see who it is who keeps pecking at the plate glass but never completing the revolution through the revolting doors.

Part 10: Nightground

When you can't sleep for walking and when there's nothing to watch but Nightmares 'til Dawn . . . when the ghosts beneath the ice-sheets are restless, gathering like ankle-bracelets at the newly-slashed soles of your feet, sit up. Take needle and thread and embroider that wound. And keep watch for his arrival.

A charming link of furless cats brings your only friend, the one who wants you for a moonbeam.

Disappointment is tangible in this narrow grove of terrors. I was reading Jeanette Winterson in the Ann Summers Sex Shop when suddenly there occurred an eclipse. I grabbed a video and pulled the slimy film out of its socket. I ran outside to look at the bashful sun and burned its message on my cranelike neck: "Secure the Shadow 'ere the Substance Fades."

Ever since, a little cloud of someone's ashes keeps following me like a pillow of salt over my left shoulder. It gets in my ears and says things like "You'll see overdone symbolism in your life/and no insight in your work/You'll be there/but you'll be forgotten."

I try to swat it away but it slips between my long fingers. It tricks me, chases me back to high school, at a big/little sister picnic held by a band shell. That amphitheater was a womb I wanted back into, believe it. So I ran in and all I can hear is this ditty about cherries and stones and chickens and bones and babies not crying and stories dragging on, lying.

I'm spat back out, pursued by these ancestral ashes, now mixed with chips and vinegar and cigarette ash, dried catsup for blood.

I tell everyone about this sketchy ghost and it becomes that when friends greet me they ask, not how are you? but how is your ghost?

It lingers often around the mouthpiece of the phone, a crop-dusting tornado, jealous.

I trap the ghost one day, in a shoebox that had held two left feet. I take the box to church to drown the ashes in holy water, but they thrive spongelike in the liquid. They blob-nudge me on to a basement bier where Monte lies in state. Even the candles must weep. Church mice tickle my bare feet: how can they be poor with so much host available?

Part 11: Sit It Out in Heaven

If these are the last words I ever write, make them the only ones I want to be remembered for: there's nothing more sexual than the London Underground. The sound, the shape, the scent, there's nothing more like sex than the Tube. As sexy as the graveyard shift and all manner of undress.

I think of Aidan in my signal-cabin fever. In a stoic brick shack and he's up there now, maybe pulling these long levers if he's not sleeping. The Ticket Inspector was just a shill, a beard. All along it was Aidan.

That I see his face when I die is all I ask of heaven.

What was between us was so tangible that it's now what keeps us apart, the way people pose by mannequins made of plaster.

I don't go to work. I go to the record store. Sonic embraces me gleefully and grasps, and gasps. "Save your strength," I tell him.

"You're a beautiful girl with a dirty mind," he says, but to me he's just someone with a chip on his shoulder the size of a tower block.

His mouth moves along my hair, and I think he must sense my distance because he says "You can think of him when you're with me." Then he pales to white as if into transparent heaven.

I suggest the phone box with the pressing ladder so we lock up shop and break for it. Throughout, though, my mind's as numb as my vagina.

This story has run out of track, become a bramble-ramble, a forum only for ghosts.

I think I may be the last of the (who cares?) geniuses scrawling on my mummy-wrap papyrus in hopes it'll keep me snug company since nothing else does.

Camden may be moving out—I keep hearing sounds to that effect. I miss my childhood hide-a-bed, and I wish I had a home to be sick for.

That night I accompany Darwin to Kensal Rise Cemetery where I break down and do it with him in the implements shed. It's so cold and mildewed I welcome the wet warmth and porridge steam. His techno tapes rage, indistinguishable from the remorseless dot-dashes of his beeper and my cowgirl yelps.

We walk hand-in-hand over the uneven night-ground and he points out peculiar memorials and broken heart tributes. He shows me desecrated doodlings, instructions for satanic bone-switching. We stop at a tree that once held a swing—now there's just a rope and a dangling wooden walk-the-plank seat.

"A busted seat's a hangman's dream," I say.

"What happens is these kids who've outgrown play come along and vandalize, because they long for it so much," he answers.

He's so sad and clear he could be beautiful. Even better, he walks on ahead of me.

I pause by the still swing now moving with the winglike kneecrest of Nell, her blown skirts revealing bother boots, the basket of matchbooks she sells providing a brake for when she chooses to stop.

At home that night I'm emptying out my wooden chest, abandoning hope like it's a sinking ship.

I ride the Underground around and around until it becomes a sight gag. I ride the tunnels in my full-length transparent C&A dress, but my Slam City Skates knapsack is full of McVitties Digestives, Walker's Crisps, Yorkie Bars, Cadbury Flakes, Birds Custard, Vimto. I consult my Ryman-slang notebook, adjust my Red or Dead shoes, and check my Hyper-Hyper watch. Yeah, me—a regular American Gothic Psycho. I unravel my antenna-plaited hair like the seam of the crime and the train grinds to a halt at Goodge Street.

No patience for the lift, I ascend, spellbound.

Lying on the kaleidoscope steps, felled in a fit of after-rave, is Aidan. His blood is a silk cravat around his mouth.

Since he's still breathing I smother and scour his soft face with my sack's sandpaper and feather pillow. A cauldron of ghosts flies up from his soul, a cutlery-array of princes from bell-towers.

We are beautifully finished.

"You'll oblige me by staying dead," I order as I hear the far-off sound of jail-guitar doors. I'm afraid of turning.

I hear voices wafting down the steps. I look up, down. Which way to climb? Underneath me a train pulls out, and as ever the wind lilts before and after in assent, in affirmation. I see Monte waving from the platform, an alluring ripple, and I dive.

(Don't Quit)
Your Day Job

*h*avoc, with her Mary Quantitative pout, is on the story again. She's seeking manna and fodder for her "Clubs and Snubs" column and trying desperately, *just this once*, to get things right. For a club/cub reporter, she's just a little too long in the tooth to grin evenly, to the right effect.

She parades her gossip like the logo that runs down the sleeve of her coveted baseball tee. But because her tales are most generally extravagantly wrong, mishaps crop up like mushroom clouds. Tonight a boy grabs her by the arm and shakes her, not as a greeting. His girlfriend AMANITA MASCARA OUT OF BLUSH was, Havoc had insisted, far from Queen of the May. She was Queen of the Definitely Will.

As the boy attempts to fragment the sentence on Havoc's sleeve, it dawns on her—like her breakfast of vodka and Froot Loops—that she'll never drink lager in this town again.

"It wasn't my fault!" she protests. "My sources were impeccable." She pauses, wondering at the word. It sounded right, plus her source was reliable: it was Alisdare, her raving-mad boyfriend who works days as a dancing chicken at a store-auction in the Finchley Road.

Alisdare had heard the story at a free-range warehouse party and then reported it along to Havoc. It had to be gospel, he'd insisted: Amanita'd even had it off with Nick Cave.

Havoc flees for home, where she nurses her arm like a suckling infant until Alisdare turns up. He smiles absently at her, fetches a can of Vimto from the fridge, and then goes to his room. He turns up the stereo while Havoc slumps in her chair. The sound from his room hits her temples like a ceaseless tennis ball bouncing against her prefab, post-Beatles dry wall.

This time it was Alisdare's mistake and he'd have to get back in her good graces. As no doubt he would: groveling comes to him naturally, hailing as he does from Crawley.

Alisdare is never in before midnight, a regular Cinderella's wayward brother. And when he is back, he is in and out of traditional consciousness so much that Havoc can't help but be drawn to him. It's a cat–and–wind-up-mouse kind of thing.

He breezes into the front room, his shirttails billowing like bunting. "We're getting a dancer for our group," he tells Havoc, puffing his chest as if he were an exotic tropical bird.

"Oh, God, why?"

Alisdare shrugs. "It's cheaper than having a light show."

"Listen, Alisdare, I have to talk to you."

"I can't now. Saints Preserve Us!"

"What?"

"We're thinking of calling the group Saints Preserve Us. That, or Manchester Martyrs."

"But aren't you all from the south?"

"That's why we'd be martyrs, heh-heh. Besides, since when are you such a stickler for detail?"

"That's what I mean, Alisdare. That's what I wanted to talk with you about." Havoc uses Alisdare's name as often and as frequently as she can, in efforts to bring him back to earth. It works about as well as stating the obvious.

"Sorry, pet, don't feel like talking right now," he says, in between bursts of telling about his plans for the group. "We'll mistake sound for feeling!" he enthuses. "We can't miss!"

The next day in the offices of the magazine she works for, Havoc huddles with her assistant, Bliss, and ponders handing in her notice. "It gets so embarrassing, Bliss, having to write things in public."

"I thought that's why you had your poison-pen name."

"No, I mean actually taking them down out there in the open. The words, I mean. People stare at you like you're doing something not exactly obscene, but really, really unsavory. And then," she pauses before continuing. "Then there's the problem of misinformation. Alisdare told me a story he swore was gospel and now it's turned out to be wrong."

"Where did he hear it?"

"I think he heard it when he was having his hair shorn, but I'm not really sure."

"He must feel sheepish," laughs Bliss while eyeing Havoc's desk and her prized pen that lights up in the dark. Bliss feels a sexy wave of envy, and of promise.

"You know, Bliss, I think I should just pack it all in. The whole Clubs and Snubs column."

"It is kind of dated. I think we should have one like *Not Drowning Raving* has."

"Yeah, maybe but I'm just not the person to do it, even though I have a ready-made source in Alisdare. I don't know; I just want to take flight!"

"Homesick? Or just peckish?"

Havoc laughs. "That's funny, coming from a girl from Peckham."

"It's still more glamorous than coming from L.A."

"But, Bliss, I'm not from L.A.! I'm from suburbia — La Milagra."

"Oh, that's all right then."

"You know, maybe I am hungry after all. Do you have time for lunch? Cranks?"

"Are you asking or accusing?"

"Both. Ready?"

Later that night, Havoc chews hungrily on the productive end of her pen. The ink coagulates against her teeth, a failed temporary filling; blue curacao confectionery. She takes notes at an event called Helium, retracing the words she'd first written in light. Habitues dance around her: sporty, spirited reformed punks and brightly-dressed recovering goths, evened out by those who'd fallen somewhere in between and then failed to get up.

At the bar, bartering for a brain drink is an acquaintance, a pliable source who, if prodded, is a font of vitriolic typeface.

"Pepsi, L–Lysine, Lucozade," Havoc butts in, to order for Jim who nods and smiles affectionately.

"Let's see," he says, knowing what's expected of him. "Oh, we have a kind of old-guard royalty here tonight. The face who launched a thousand sad plaid shirts, a thousand little sh—Smiths fans. I know you don't like profanity, Hav."

"Thanks. Morrissey's here?"

"The moaning cavern himself."

"Celibate still?"

"Celibate never! The things I could tell you." Jim swallows a pill with his drink. "Have to watch my e-numbers."

"You're saying he's not celibate?"

"Get thee to a nunnery! Never has been, never will."

"Morrissey not celibate," murmurs Havoc. And then, louder: "Now, this is something to celebrate!" She stirs Jim's drink with her fountain pen.

"I only have a moment, though," he confides. "I have to get lucky tonight."

Havoc smiles as she puts the varnishing touches on

her column. It's so self-satisfying; like buffing her nails.

. . . Something to celibate. For those of you who still think former top-pop-fop and all around shy-guy Morrissey carries an Atlas-style tortoise-shell on his back (and not just as eyewear), Havoc say RELAX. That's no shell, that's a mattress. The 1980s foremost moaning cavern has slept his way around the world. He's one stalactite who stalag-might, ALWAYS . . .

. . . And in the reformed punks and recovering goths department, still spelunking, we find Nick Cave. Well, Nick hasn't done anything, really. Nick doesn't have to . . .

. . . Which legendary member of the punk-rock Bromley Contingent seems sitting pretty to tell all in a tower-blockbusting soon to be best-seller/dweller? And which lucky columnist, dear readers, is poised to be her ghost? Well, this is one ghost-writer who wants in spelled out in sky-writing: it's yours truly. And the once baby-Brommer is . . .

. . . turn in early next week. And until then, Enjoy life: Eat Out More Often . . .

Days later, after the magazine has graced newsstands and dominated placards [New *SEEN* Out Now] Havoc sits at her desk, pining for mail to open. Her intercom bleats, and she is summoned to her editor's office.

Felix Huft is an Austrian so fair you need ski glasses just to glance at him. He's fair, too, as editors go: when his writers fail to give him what he wants, he

doesn't rant; he simply scolds tenderly and construc-
tively suggests. When he demands the realistically
impossible — and his staff balks — Felix simply tilts his
head to one side like a sandy-colored Labrador puppy.
Then his group empathizes, and over-achieves.

Except for Havoc, that is. Havoc, who is decidedly
feline. She sits down in Felix's office, in his Breuer
chair, and still she maintains the perfect posture she
earned in charm school.

"How are you, Havoc?" Felix begins. "I just need a
word, a moment of your time." He pauses. "This story
of yours about Morrissey, it has made us look rather
silly."

"Us? You should see him!"

"I appreciate your humor, but you must take more
care to verify things. Then there was your item about
Nick Cave."

"Pardon me, but there can't be anything wrong with
that one."

"True. But it's so fawning, Havoc. It's so fawning
it could have been written by Bambi."

"Bambi's mother," Havoc corrects.

Felix tilts his head but Havoc remains statue-still.
She knows he is about to issue a warning.

"I must warn you . . . "

Havoc doesn't listen; instead she imagines she is
effortlessly scooping Felix's blue eyes out of their sockets, and placing them on the ground where she'll toy
with them as if they were marbles. When it seems like
he's through talking, Havoc politely excuses herself.

Soon, at work, Havoc (whose response to criticism is denial and retreat) becomes sloppy in her usually trendy demeanor. Her style has gone the way of all flesh: ashen. Her hair is stringy and greasy-spoon dishwater brown; her clothes, sackcloth. The circles around her eyes are like Saturn's rings; her freckles its fog-clouded moons.

To Bliss she hisses, so much so that her tough assistant is reduced to tears at least three times a day.

"Stiff upper lip!" Havoc commands. "What's wrong with you? Crying's for nurseries!"

Isn't that what this is? thinks Bliss. The Little Shop of Horrors?

"It isn't even as if she is clever anymore," Bliss confides to Oscar, the postboy, while she's fetching Havoc's coffee.

"Don't cry, love," Oscar reassures. "Well, cry if it makes you feel better. But it's better still to get even."

Bliss smiles, ignorant no longer.

"I just heard an interesting thing," Bliss offers to Havoc, along with the coffee. Havoc is making an Advent calendar on her desk blotter, using Post-It Notes and club-society photos. It makes up the grounds surrounding her house built out of calling cards.

"It's about Billy Bragg," Bliss continues.

"He's not news," Havoc spits, sibilantly.

"He is when he comes out in favor of reinstating Margaret Thatcher."

Havoc knocks over her card house with one fell

swoop of her wrecking-balled fist. Inside, trouble
dolls lay together *in flagrante.*

"Havoc, that's hilarious!" Bliss points, awed.

"You're sure about this?"

"I've never been wrong."

"You've also never fed me anything before."

"Except lunch." And there's no such thing as a free
one, Bliss grins, to herself.

"You're an angel, an absolute cherub," Havoc
praises, retrieving her laptop Mac from beneath a
stack of teen magazines.

. . . The Bard of Barking, Billy (I'm not one to)
Bragg, that lovable lefty; that hound has found another camp in which to bask, far from his usual laborious
roost. He's agitating for the return to power of Mrs.
Thatcher. This, readers, is one former chicken who
just might catch a Tory vote of confidence. Yes, there
just might be some strength in THIS union . . .

. . . And speaking of more perfect unions, let's
not forget the upcoming nuptials of Wedding Present
figurehead David Gedge. Now, what to gift this guy
with? Maybe one-time Birthday Party guitarist
Rowland Howard? Or perhaps Roland Gift? After all
it is a WEDDING. Give the guy something he can
use! . . .

Havoc smiles conspiratorially, confidently.

. . . Nick Cave, dear readers, still doesn't have to
do anything . . .

. . . and don't forget to watch for my upcoming
opus, co-written with Sue Animal Crackers, *Punk*

Soup. It'll set straight any preconceived sewing notions you might have that punks were all sexless monsters. You'll be like Frankenstein's creation . . . IN STITCHES!

. . . Until then, ENJOY LIFE, etc . . .

"Stitched up, more like," Bliss smiles as she proofreads Havoc's column. Havoc has left uncharacteristically early, to accompany Alisdare to a Rave on Ice.

The Grave Rave on Ice is anything but. That is to say, it's on ice all right, but it's not severity but levity that is thematic.

Oswald "Lucky" Flowers leaves his perpetual date, supermodel Inky Tree, and makes a beeline for Havoc, who's just emerged from the powder room. "I looked so pale," she explains to Oswald, "that I had to add some blood-orange blush to my cheeks." Havoc's brown hair sheens sweaty black, and a copper comb slips precariously toward the nape of her neck.

They dance, quick isolated stills twenty-four-to-a-second. Their arms fan each other into flattery, to a jerky song by the Prodigy.

"How old are you?" Oswald asks Havoc.

"You first."

"Oh, my age varies with the situation."

They continue to dance as ice melts from overhead orbs, falling in icicle-sized feathers.

Beneath their feet the ice cracks and splits, an unfortunate magic mirror. But Havoc and Oswald don't notice; they just carry on in time to the thumping rhythms. When the floor finally separates to reveal a swimming hole, they let the rest of the crowd fall in.

Oswald pushes Havoc toward a far corner of the hall and pleads with her there for a kiss. Havoc shoves him away.

"I'm only dancing," she admonishes, before careening away and then playfully hiding behind a refrigerator-sized block of ice.

The block is shaded at its core, like the joke-ice her parents used to trick their cocktail guests with. Inside the tiny plastic square would be a burnt match or plastic fly—hilarious.

This block has what must be a huge model of a fly, Havoc surmises. On the side is a number: 12.15.66, and a signature with an *i* dotted like bubbles gasping for air.

It is a logo as unmistakable as that of a particularly imperialist corporation.

Havoc knows who is inside as sure as any girl who'd spent her free-formative years in La Milagra—or indeed anywhere in America—would. It's the man who rendered the remainder of her world, from history-thick castles to sugar-frosted mountains, nothing more than a surrogate Disneyland.

Havoc gasps. She has the scoop of the century.

She stumbles back to the reinstated dance floor, flooded now with drenched swimmers writhing to Carter the Unstoppable Sex Machine's "101 Damnations."

Havoc looks, she panics. She can't find anyone she knows that she trusts.

She hunts and pecks for Alisdare.

"I knew you'd return," says Lucky as he locks Havoc in the fleshy jail of his arms.

She ducks her escape. "Have you seen Alisdare?"

"I don't think he's here," announces Inky, who appears suddenly, like a surprise victory.

"But he'd never leave this early!"

Inky laughs. "Maybe he's turning over a new leaf."

Havoc leaves the ice rink and searches for a cab. There aren't any, for she's in Barnet.

A phone, perhaps?

It's so early the pubs are open, taking last orders.

Havoc pushes her way through smoke as impenetrable as dry ice; she heads for the phone, a trophy in the back.

She phones home.

No answer.

She phones Bliss and gets an answering machine.

"Bliss, it's Hav. I'm in Edgware—Barnet, I mean. I—I have a story. The story. The biggest story ever. If you were in, I'd ask you to come and meet me. No, better still. I know what I need now. I need a photographer. I'll speak to you later."

Havoc hangs up and calls Kevin, a surly bear. He growls his hibernating hello.

"Kev, it's Havoc. I need you right away. There's a shot you HAVE to get!"

"If it's not Joy Division or the Sex Pistols I don't want to know." Kevin hangs up.

Havoc struggles to regain her professional composure. She starts to cry.

"There, there," booms a voice from behind, an uneasy conscience. Havoc turns to brush against a young man with a Spartacus haircut. He offers to buy her a drink.

"Is everyone from Los Angeles as attractive as you?" he asks, appraising her accent.

She nearly bolts. "I'm not from there," she corrects. "I'm from a place called La Milagra."

"I know it!" the lad, who's called Gez, shouts. "It's by Disneyland!"

"How about that drink?" Havoc asks, certain now she's found someone she can trust.

"A snakebite for the lady Eve," Gez barks.

"That's not my name."

"It's a joke, love."

Havoc gulps the sickly concoction and leans on Gez. "How do you feel about a rave?"

"Your place or mine?"

"No, serious. Close to here."

"I'm right inside you," he winks, but she ignores it.

There are flashing lights and blipping sounds outside the Grave Rave—unmistakable side effects of a raid.

"Oh, no!" Havoc screams. "I have to go in there!" She grabs Gez's arm and pulls it as if it is a rope in a tug-of-war.

"Suit yourself," answers a soft-spoken policeman. "But if you go in, you're coming out and along with us."

She stampedes in and slides through the soggy medicinal hall, toward the corner in question. It's empty: not even a clue is left behind.

Gez pulls away. "I'm off. The last place I want to go is inside."

"That's not what you said earlier," Havoc reminds, throwing down his arm. Gez disappears out a back door and hovers by a skip until the coast is clear.

But Havoc, dumbstruck, keeps standing in the same spot.

"It has to be here."

"Come along," another, less genteel, policeman says.

"Don't touch me!"

In a holding cell with several hapless ravers, Havoc complains.

"Can I at least have something to read?"

"You outcasts is all alike!" laughs a jailer. "Always moaning about something."

◻◼◻◼

Havoc, out of jail and alone in her flat, obstinately refuses to sulk. Her job is gone, her boyfriend along with it. He languishes in Bliss's camp as the chief trooper.

But Hav has other things on her mind. For one, to-

day's book-signing, a task-and-treat she shares with
the woman who keeps treading on Havoc's shadow,
Sue Animal Crackers.

Sue will read, Havoc will write the majority of the
dedications: the reader's name, her own, and a taw-
dry, tired ampersand waiting for Sue's hasty scrawl.

Sue provides the flourish. Her pasty skin looks like
fried bread before it hits the grill, and her hair, once
renowned for ending in feline fists, is now as soft and
sullen as a back-combed beauty queen's.

She wears a dark, straight wool-induced dress that
dejectedly meets her faceless knees.

Her shoes, on sandalwood legs, are flat and long.

She looks like she should be pushing a Southwark
pram instead of a book.

Havoc struggles in her high-chair stool in her place
behind the counter; she adjusts her inappropriate
cleavage inside a tinsel-streaked Westwood corset.

THE DAZE OF THE LOW CUTS, notes Bliss, who
doesn't stay.

"When my mother told me to close my eyes and
think of England, I obeyed," begins Sue. "I shut them
tight to blot out her horrid middle-class parlor. And
I saw tower blocks, attached to boys with names like
Berlin. Like Two-tone Steve and Nils. Sid Vicious.

"I left my safe suburban home for the comforts of
Louise's Soho bar. And I never looked back.

"Till now." Sue sighs, finding her pace.

"Move in closer," she requests of the motley throng
scattered throughout the maze-like bookstore.

"I want to tell you something."

She smiles, and suddenly she's not Georgie Girl but Julie Christie.

"In the first place, why do you think he was called Ten-Pole Tudor?"

The crowd laughs. They embrace her with their will.

Havoc wanders off, mentally. She looks distractedly at the crowd and settles her gaze on three weighty women—meddling good fairies with the menacingly well-wishing faces of Main Street, USA.

She feels herself transported along with them, as stubborn and unwilling as a cart on a theme-ride track. She's not drifting off smoothly but putting up a hopeless stubborn struggle.

Havoc awakens in a slump, in a one-room apartment in Los Angeles. She parts the dirty glass curtains as if they were her long greasy bangs and strains to read the street sign, Laurelei Drive. A cross street is obscured by a lint-encrusted palm tree, an outsized overblown waiting wish of a dandelion.

The room is completely furnished for her: even the keys are arranged in a loving array on the Early American dining room table. Its legs are swollen arthritic joints of knotty wood.

Havoc goes outside, with the idea of sending a telegram. Instead she's distracted by the neighboring home, an imposing mansion that looks down on her tiny, stucco-honeycomb building. It creates a moldy shade that smothers her astroturf lawn, her meteor-showered roof. The house has three turrets and a heavily thatched roof—even surly Santa Anas couldn't blow it down.

Sunset Boulevard is several craggy blocks away, so Havoc rethinks. Maybe there's a phone in her apartment.

There is, of course. A cat-curled princess one.

She dials Western Union, to send a phonegram to Gez.

"Don't worry," she dictates. "Everything okay. Will give details when arrive."

Gez, answering his phone, could care.

Havoc's refrigerator is stocked with frozen fare from an offbeat local market.

EAT ME, reads a carrot cake, so she obeys.

A few hours later, she wakes up rested. Who knows what visions plummeted in her sleeping mind: intrepid rabbits, glue-sniffing run-of-the-milliners, poker-faced card carriers . . . they're all lost to Havoc now as she assesses her condition.

She approaches the phone again and dials Information to get the number of the *National Intruder*.

The receptionist at the publication dutifully listens to Havoc's scoop.

"Okay, there are several things wrong," she informs Havoc after she finally reaches her breathless break.

"First of all, it is a myth that Walt Disney was frozen, so if what you say is true, it must be someone else that you saw.

"Secondly, we would never give credence to a story

originating from a drugged whoop-dee-doo in London."

"Why not?" asks Havoc, wavering between shame and outrage.

She hangs up and then searches her closet for suitable attire to wear to Disneyland. The wardrobe is perfect: broken-in Levi's, roomy tees, deck shoes.

Havoc showers and dresses, then leaves her apartment to go to the carport. A pleasant-faced woman is out in front of the mansion house; she waves enthusiastically at Havoc, who waves back.

In her alloted parking space sits a tiny Autopian convertible. It starts when she gets in it, and Havoc heads east and then south for Disneyland.

Havoc overshoots her destination, distracted by a glaring, blinding cathedral, an array of Grim Reaper topiary shrubs, a globe skewered by a large cocktail toothpick, and a crematorium that most resembles a California mission.

These are the familiars of Havoc's La Milagra childhood.

She aims for Santa Ana's Fourth Street, for a bar her father often threatened to substitute in place of a touted visit to the Magic Kingdom, a seedy side-street dive called Dizzyland.

Nine old men prop up the bar; aside from the bartender, Havoc is the only woman.

"I'll have a pint—I mean a glass of, ah, Pabst Blue Ribbon, please," Havoc requests softly and the woman, a beer-bottle brunette, turns to draw it.

"Hop to it, Jinda," says a man, Tom, who laughs alone.

Havoc looks at him—his tony clothes and preppy L.L.-Bean-of-Main-Street demeanor make him distinct in this crowd who wear what look like bibs made out of bar coasters.

Havoc gravitates toward him—he could be the American counterpart to Gez—another disinterested confidante.

"Hi, my name's Tom," he says, extending his free hand. "As in Tomorrowland."

"Havoc, as in habitual."

To Havoc's controlled disbelief, Tom tells her of his vocation, that of Imagineer. "It is a vocation," he underscores, running his index finger along the slippery bar. "A calling, a religious devotion. And they've rewarded me with the keys to the city, so to speak."

"What do you mean?"

"What I mean is that when the park is closed to Mr. and Mrs. Snerd of Hobo Valley and their three rebellious children, it's open to me."

Havoc reaches for her pocket watch. "Like now, for instance?"

"Let's see, it's open 'til midnight tonight, which means at 12:01, it's all ours. Our oyster. Did you know that Walt intended for Disneyland never to be completed?"

"Sounds like a bid for immortality."

"Oh, I think he's pretty safe there." Tom drains his glass mug.

"What do you mean?"

"You say that a lot. I just mean it's a pretty safe bet that the Disney legend will endure."

Havoc pictures a safe, all right, the block of ice he's encased in. Still she keeps mum.

"Ready to go, Havoc?" Tom asks.

"How come you didn't balk at my name?"

"When you're dealing with Dopey, Sleepy, Sneezy, and Dumbo it's not that unusual." He smiles, the impish fresh-faced twist of a cloyingly defiant Norman Rockwell child. When Havoc takes his arm, he blushes straight down to the neckline of his red-check shirt.

To be inside the park is like being mired in a box of Havoc's grandmother's costume jewelry. At the end of one strand, like a decorative medallion, is the stilted House of the Future.

In Tomorrowland, flying saucers bounce and bobble like clip-on earrings on animated lobes.

Clearly, Havoc is inside the Magic Kingdom of yesterday.

On Main Street, Tom and Havoc observe leeches writhing in an apothecary jar.

"I'm not really a fan of Main Street," Havoc protests. "It always makes me think of Gopher Prairie." She pictures the ominous faces of the three interfering fairies, who got her into this predicament.

"Let's go somewhere else," Tom consoles, chivalrous.

They head for Monsanto's Adventures in Inner Space: Better Living Through Chemistry.

"I remember this ride!" Havoc enthuses. "In fact, in London, where I work, I once did an interview with this band called the Dark Ride. And I told them about this ride, and about how I lost a portion of my virginity on it."

Tom shifts, appears uncomfortable.

"But, being English, the band couldn't quite grasp what I meant."

They board the half-shell cars and strain to find their reflections, pearl-sized and miniaturized, before they get off.

"I can't believe you didn't try to kiss me," Havoc chides. "Now, that's a first for me."

"Let's go to Tom Sawyer's Island."

The ride operator greets Tom pleasantly and beams equally at Havoc as they drift sideways toward the tiny cement island.

In Injun Joe's Cave Tom confesses, "I think Walt's buried in here somewhere. I think he's the treasure that's being protected."

"Oh, I beg to differ! He's frozen!"

"And never the twain shall meet," booms a voice, before a large, jovial man steps out from behind a stalagmite.

"Kay," Tom greets. "How are you doing? Listen, meet my friend, Havoc."

"Pleasure, Havoc," says Kay, as he holds onto her hand just a fraction, a silly millimeter too long. He looks at her as if she were a prized antique cameo and he an avid collector. He is both intimately familiar and entirely awestruck.

"Well, I'll leave you two alone," Kay allows. "I was just taking a little spin around the park before I turned in."

"Nice to have met you," Havoc says, meaning the opposite. When he's gone, she asks Tom, "What does he do?"

"Kay? He's a merchandiser."

"Oh."

"What's your favorite toy?"

"It wasn't one I had, but one I saw in the toy museum in Bethnal Green. It was this immaculate rag doll with the most beautiful face, dressed in this lulling fabric. I'll just never forget it."

"The interesting thing about rag dolls is that the ones that survived intact are the ones that weren't favored, weren't played with."

"I never thought of it like that before. So this gorgeous creature was unloved. That's so poignant."

Tom takes her hand, as bashful as a backward date.

"Or is it," Havoc continues, "that the things which endure weren't really loved?"

"Maybe just too precious to touch."

Havoc and Tom leave the park, and due to the hour, check into the Space Age Motel.

They sleep apart, adrift, like tiny gems in king-sized settings.

In the morning Havoc goes to the lobby to get some

coffee granules for the coffeemaker that's perched next to the towel rack in their bathroom.

She spies a new issue of the *National Intruder* with her scoop cutting a wide swath across its cover.

A sidebar tells of Kay's plans to sell little Walts in blocks of plastic cocktail ice, in finer Houses of Humor everywhere.

Havoc rushes back to their room and drags Tom out of bed and down the steps as if he is a cherished teddy bear.

◻■■

In London, Bliss has just renamed the column she inherited "Bird on a Wire." She checks the news-service teletype avidly and is curious to learn of Havoc's newest story.

"For those still interested in the travails of this space's former scribe—the same who was last seen fleeing a book-signing of a tomb, ah tome, she'd publicly ghosted, leaving her co-author as stranded as a Roxy Music damsel—here's the latest: she claims she's found the preserved remains of Walt Disney. As in Dumbo. Is her story as airtight as his slumber pad? Don't count on it: the most famous public stiff since Lenin (not that one) simply can't be on the half-shell at a North London rave.

"It's a good bet Havoc-kins will be shedding beaucoup mouse-ke-tears over this debacle.

"It's hard to chart the decline of this former star-spotter, but it would appear she went from a sort of shut-eye diplomacy to dipsomania in a single fell swoop. I mean, lately more people have seen her down the pub than they have Glen Matlock. And you know that's saying a mug-full."

▢■▢

Havoc is back in her Lorelei abode, staring catlike out the window. She spies her neighbor tending some lilies that border the shaded walk approaching her home. The woman waves Havoc down.

"I'm Sheilah," she says, extending a padded, garden-gloved hand.

"Havoc."

"Charmed, Havoc." Sheilah's accent has the same lyrical lilt as Havoc's. "You're my new neighbor."

"It's too elaborate, how I got here," Havoc dismisses. "Are you from London too?"

"I am indeed," Sheilah laughs, all twinkle-bell sparkle like Billie Burke. "I escaped the East End. But why don't I tell you my tale over coffees, say, about quarter to five?"

"Okay. Should I bring anything?"

"Could you manage some Hershey bars?"

"Okay," says Havoc, tentatively. She'd rather eat mud.

"Let's make it a quarter to four instead," Sheilah suggests. "Did you know that's the time clock faces are most often set to, before they're sold?"

"No, I didn't," Havoc half smiles, stunted by this bit of useless information. "See you then."

Havoc walks along the Sunset Strip to Turner's Liquor Store, where she purchases the candy. She stops inside a book shop on the way back, but *Punk Soup* is not for sale. Instead, displayed like doughnuts stacked on cake trays are copies of *Beloved Infidel*.

From inside the shop Havoc looks out at the street; the cars there are big and round and the traffic lights shift more slowly. Norma Desmond drifts by, chauffeured by her husband. Some lucky fool got his pool.

Havoc rushes outside and once again the Strip is as dissonant and desperate as "MTV Unplugged." She gazes across the street at Tower Records, which boasts a billboard advertising *Punk Soup*. Havoc goes inside and, embarrassed, buys a copy which she places in her knapsack. Then she flees for home, where she stays inside until it's time to visit Sheilah.

Sheilah's home has all the darkness of paneled wood offset by shadows cast by a large fire behind an ornamental grate. Havoc sits on a brocade couch, herself as awkward as its stubby carved legs.

"My story is this," Sheilah begins. "I am an orphan who worked my way out of the slums. I did every job I could—addressograph girl, toothbrush demonstrator, showgirl. Anything to escape my life. In one of my foster homes I had a doll I could look at but was forbidden to play with. That doll, my dear, looked just like you."

Havoc turns her head, uncertain how to react.

"Eventually I bettered myself," continues Sheilah. "I became a gossip columnist for the *Hollywood Recorder*. Here, let me read you one of my pieces."

Sheilah begins. To Havoc's horror, her writing is every bit as drab and lackluster as Bliss's attempts.

"Did you want some of the Hershey bars?" Havoc ventures, when Sheilah's finished reading. "I bought the box of six." She reaches into her knapsack.

"No, dear," Sheilah grins. "I want you to have them." The firelight transforms her; she is as grim as Snow White's single parent.

"I don't really eat American chocolate," Havoc wards off. "But do you have time for my story?"

"Of course."

Havoc spins her yarn, tapping her foot to stress certain points.

"I believe you," Sheilah consoles. "Not only that, but I would gladly print your entire story. I intend to, in fact. The only problem being that I write solely in the past."

Havoc looks down as the fire crackles. Its logs are rolled-up copies of the *National Intruder* and the *Hollywood Recorder*. Sheilah fans a copy of *Beloved Infidel* so that its covers touch, making a childhood-craft miniature Christmas tree. She tosses it into the flames.

Reaching into her sack, Havoc retrieves *Punk Soup*. It resists catching fire at first, like a brick might, but soon it catches on. It creates so many sparks they rival the cursor on her Mac as she's back in her London office, polishing off another "Clubs and Snubs" column.

. . . Deep in the jungles of Brazil Nick Cave has found a cure for despair. It's a rare fruit called dispare, or something like that. Who cares . . .

She files her nails on the embossed edges of her engraved invitation to the much-touted marriage of Amanita Mascara and Morrissey. Abjectly, Havoc wonders if silver ice molds in the shapes of a zealous animator would be an appropriate wedding gift.

Stiletto
Life

*i*n a world not quite like this one, Gene Plantagenet and his faithless sidekick, Colonel Candlestick, went through their emotionless routine down at the Black Drop, a pub so named for its flock-dusted wallpaper, corpuscle-red yet choked with ash residue.

In other words, black and red like propaganda.

Gene lived alone near Greenwich Park in a ghastly flat that was far too elaborate. So overdone was it that it was more decoy than decor.

Because Gene had something to hide, but he couldn't. It was a physical part of him, a combination Eiffel/Bloody Tower done in cartilage form.

He was neither French nor royal but who's counting.

Colonel Candlestick visited him at home from time to time, always invited the way some Invisible think they are. His was a standing stiff, formal invitation, much like the man himself. Correspondingly, his and Gene's rag-and-bone man act was as far from being passion-basted as Gene had to be.

"I love you," Gene had said in his sleep just before his girlfriend walked out on him.

"Congratulations," she replied, waking him. "You've progressed. You're telling lies to the pillows now."

Gene looked not at her but at his backward book collection, spines pressed shyly against the wall, cornered.

He shrugged her off, aware the world was divided into two kinds of people: haunted or, no.

When he was younger, at the age where one experiences either love or visions, he fell prey to the latter. "I can see inside your mind where even dreams are blue," he said to Hannah, his first attempted kiss. She shoved him away.

Still in bed, he surveyed the ceiling's pre-Raphaelite pets which were fore-postered there. On the walls, myriad mirrors had tinfoil or gilt edges, and bordering velvet paintings tackled the life of Christ.

When it came to art, Gene didn't even know what he liked.

In his early twenties he decided to change the margins of his life from wide to erratic so it would be more like poetry.

In short, he became a rebellious nuisance.

That is, until *it* happened.

As a result, girls can't be let close. One woman got

the idea to explore Gene during his sleep. What she found made her draw back in horror: his nocturnal emissions, you see, were anthropomorphic. They were portland moon-stones made transparent flesh.

In a world and a time entirely free of diseases that decimate, leave it to Gene to have his own set of problems.

The girl pressed Kleenex to the residue on his thighs and the tissue stuck in wads 'til he was left to look like a Sunday school construction-paper angel.

Factor in Gene's morbid fear of insomnia, which he was certain was triggered by the sound of trains calling distantly and dispassionately in the night. He realized then why people frequented night clubs—to stamp away and stave off the inevitable.

But there were nights when it just didn't sit right to sleep alone. He would cross and uncross his arms over his chest, candy-cane sepulchre-style. Anything to conduit. Anything to connect.

Abashedly he'd wander out to pubs and pick up pint glasses with lipstick prints smeared on them. And he'd linger on the greasy crescents, certain it was the closest he'd ever get to a kiss.

He'd be jeopardized, however, if he got recognized.

"I'll lift you up," he'd promise a girl drawn to him as if to a flickering t.v. screen in a darkened room. "I'll lift you up not with wings but with magnets."

She'd giggle and wiggle, wink and sink. Before bed that night they'd play spin the poison bottle—its

ribbed rim the only lips they'd meet, gulped secretions
the sole ablution.

In bed alone he'd sleep that night, all right and tight
as a mummy.

Unless, of course, he felt like exposing himself to
haunting her.

In which case, for the girl, one damsel who'd make
him break down and cry, the consequences would be
as ominous as seeing a sky whose comforting blanket-
rule was overrun, was spoilt, by uneven planets, as
unwelcome in this world's sky as stars are in ours.

◻▮▮

Together Gene and the Colonel have an act called
Clueless, a mock-turtle rubbernecked bored game
based on the Parker Brothers diversion.

Gene gathers most of his material while in the tub,
knowing that the best bath always requires the corresponding state of mind. Still he's an insatiable worri-
er, a pointillist perfectionist, about his work.

He and Colonel launch into their routine about
mood hair, and in performance it has the success rate
of spinning gold into straw. But being more decon-
structionists than alchemists, they persist. They wear
out the skit at the Black Drop, where the audience is,
they decide, as perplexed as plastic. They are, Gene
sourly chides, Parasites Lost.

But he ignores the hecklers while he turns his head
to ingest a drug called Anathema. By the time he and

Colonel concede the stage, Gene's stars have borne out.

The bartender summons an angry Gene, the former declaring that there's a telephone call for him. Gene glares his refusal, inciting and insisting that if a phone has a cradle, then it also has a grave.

"It's the press," the barkeep persists, and Gene pictures the device that parts flower petals for arid, loveless posterity. He forward-marches to greet the phone.

A reporter named Havoc burbles her enthusiasm like an overflowing bath and Gene agrees to meet her later in the Dip, a South London landscape densely haunted and named for what people used to do on the dance floor. He spies her near a dirty frozen pond, the exact color of the concrete that banks it.

Havoc waylays him and it circumvents confrontation of his problem. They head for a warehouse event called Intolerance. During a song sampling "Voodoo Chile," Havoc bites his ample, amplified earlobe.

" 'I'm doing a story about a woman who has these casts of sixties rock stars', um, *things*,' " she says, as if quoting someone else. " 'Hendrix's is one of them, but there's no way to prove it.' "

"It would be rather difficult to authenticate," Gene responds. "I think it was Napoleon who was castrated and the search for his grail followed him much *beyond* the grave."

"Plaster of Paris, indeed!"

In bed alone that night Gene applies Havoc's information like a poultice to his sorry life.

The next day Gene is pretty-boy sure he shouldn't see Havoc again and indeed desire is usually like a dud-drug that never quite kicks in. The fire doesn't work; he thinks it mustn't.

But something in Gene must stray: he's like the pet who's left his collar, snidely and narrowly, on an accusing tree limb. So he makes a date of Havoc's choosing, to see an all-girl group called Synapse Dragons who boast a lead singer, Pola, who's always in her blew-it period.

Angry, that's all.

As a safety net Gene brings Colonel along.

Pola's hypertension alloys Gene, whose internal clock seldom wavers from Greenwich Mean Time. Thus he feels compelled to harass her, to harness her in his control (often akin to that of a headless horseman's).

"The singer's not the song," Havoc reassures him. "The same can be applied to religion." Gene takes the opportunity to offer up a silent prayer: "Oh, God, whatever you might be, siphon out my spirit if thou wilst, and then leave me alone!"

Apart from Havoc, another American is at large in the club, as reinvented as Havoc herself or anyone who's escaped from their childhood bed. The venue plays host to Olive, another ex-pat off her back, for the moment anyway. Olive cares not at all for the music and hasn't for eternities—at least six *NME*'s—but she likes the errant rhythms of the pirating Dragons. She likes how they hate; a dying art in pop music.

Olive is as lost as anyone has a right to be, xenophobic zippers at her ankles and laddering her crotch. She wears stretch pants styled for the slopeless and has a broken heart propped up as a broken leg might be.

"I don't know how it happened," she confesses to Pola, "or even who's responsible." She shakes her head as though trying to loosen some memory, "the pull of something remembering me."

Poor Olive. Her body belongs to both sides.

Pola brings up the lead onstage where she vents and rants. Havoc takes notes, but the serifs on her characters lean so far into the preceding word that it's either an obliteration or homage to an unwanted past.

In reality she wants to write poetry.

◻◼◼

What's missing from these lives apart from the now-obligatory things-they'll-never-have is mo-men-tum. Ho-hum. Never mind the end of their millennium: what they need is the end of all their world.

◻◼◼

Gene nods along with Havoc's cute remarks, secretly planning ahead how to avoid sex. He errs, you know. His peculiar ectoplasm, once ejaculated, is a no more beautiful spirit than could ever be found. It's one hundred percent. It often sticks to his proof-sheets like a better-grade cellophane, but if it breaks free and takes on a life of its own overnight, like Silly Putty out of its plastic egg, there's no one who can escape its liberty-unleashing print. And find themselves bested for it, with interest.

Still, he'd sooner the avoidance tactic, best obtained by telling jokes. He miscalculates: a woman's deepest desire is only to be haunted.

He leaves Colonel with conversing duties to Havoc, which are minimal considering there's a band on, and wanders abstractly yet objectively around the club. Gene starts when he sees Olive, who's ordering a drink. Her voice: it's the sound of someone picking up the phone on a late Friday afternoon and trying to disguise any betrayal that she desperately wishes she were speaking to someone else. It has that hurt, yet polite, sorrow.

Gene makes way for her to carry her drink, cups his hand as a beer mat. He's afraid to leave her side, just as he'd be afraid to turn off the radio after he'd found the station he'd always dreamed of and could sense was there, but was equally sure that once he'd tuned out, he'd discover it never really existed at all. It was a prank of phantom airwaves.

A voltage-bolt Pola receives from the microphone knocks her band and the crowd to the ground. When Gene, Olive, Havoc, and Colonel recover, their arms are stiff and made from a kind of durable, flesh-colored plastic. Collecting themselves, each discovers the shock of the nude, for they are.

They scramble for the club's feeble dressing room and enter the tiny cubicles. It's an astoundingly good sign that the clothes closets are at least twice the size of the changing stalls. Olive slips into a strapless, body-smothering gold brocade dress and slides her arched feet into open-toed, stiletto mules. Havoc settles on a cheerleader's outfit, the sweater of which is emblazoned with a large *M*. It's about all that's alloted her.

Gene and Colonel emerge in fifties sports shirts and chinos, and are decidedly dull apart from their plastic yellow Oxfords which have shoelaces patterned into the mold. All parties have gained about four inches and the girls survey their ample busts. Havoc, for one, is annoyed, never having desired firm, pointy high-C's. "They make me feel trite," she mourns, in her cups.

And the men have their own problems, apart from their dire clothing. Their chests are flat and fit, but then, so is their sex. Make that *no* sex. As in the organ grinder must have some grist for *his* mill. Gene is cautiously elated . . .

When they all meet at the bar, it becomes evident they are the only ones standing. Havoc, the most astute more by necessity than nature, knows precisely what's happened. "We've all become Barbie dolls," she relates. "You're Barbie," she tells Olive. "You're

Ken, Gene. And Colonel here is Alan, Ken's mutant, *mute* sidekick."

"Cheers," says Colonel, who never says anything. "And who does that make you?"

"It's too horrid. I'm *Midge*." Havoc fears the mirror, that she might look to find a flock of freckles on her formerly healthless skin.

"What are we going to do about it?" Olive asks.

"Wh-who says we have to do anything?" Gene stammers.

"I do!" Olive stamps her straight, ruler-length leg and Gene is rendered helpless.

"There must be something . . . " says Havoc, who is clever and has some experience in these things. "First of all, let's go."

Parked prominently in front of the club is a huge plastic convertible with room to move two. It's obviously Olive's car. She motions to Gene to get in and he does. They drive to her apartment.

Havoc and Colonel simply shrug at each other and go their separate ways. Lives are not a luxury readily allowed them.

Havoc's flat is a fashion-showroom, a lot she accepts for now, aware she'll put things rife in the morning. She discards her letter-girl sweater and her full red corduroy skirt (it settles on the floor to look like a bean-bag chair). Then she pulls off her tennies and tube socks, and dons cotton pajamas before climbing in to sleep in a kind of trundle bed.

Olive and Gene sleep together, side by immobile side.

In the morning Havoc puts on a strawberry-colored terrycloth robe decorated with a tiny *m* and dares the mirror. Her hair, which she feels to be in a flip with eyebrow-teasing bangs, appears as Medusa-curls and complements her snake-eyes. She searches the cupboards and finds wigs, falls, and hairpieces, none of which is meant for her. Further exploration reveals iron-to-sew dresses and scores of earrings and shoes, but nothing that helps her.

Then she looks in the showcase: inside are a dozen plaster-casts of members, each labeled in magic marker at its base. Jimi Hendrix, Noel Redding, Napoleon, Robert Plant. A tiny bell rings, as if pulled by a parakeet, heralding someone's arrival in her home, the shop. Havoc looks to find a wild-eyed young woman with sneezy, cayenne-colored hair and flat feet. She wears a red and black skating costume and her muff is whitest white.

"I'm Cynthia," the youth announces. "And I've come to pick up my objets d'art." She motions toward the showcase. And Havoc, as the reliable Midge, gains the famed groupie's confidence as she recounts her life as a plaster-caster.

☐■■

The Black Drop's backdrop is different as Gene and Colonel take the stage. Gone is the familiar encrusted

velveteen: it's been replaced by happy-go-lucky paisley and shamrock. It doesn't bode well for their routine, trading as it does off Doom.

"The Lazy Fair" is a new skit they've developed about
indifferent carneys and the consequences. "They're not
barkers, they're woofers," Gene announces, detailing
the catastrophe aboard the fareless wheel.

"And now for all the ladies and Germs fans," he
continues, "here's a listing of this week's most unlikely
double-bills. The other day I chanced upon the odd
pairing of Discharge and DeBarge. Guns n' Roses and
the Stone Roses. Bauhaus and acid house. Pale Saints
and Utah Saints." The jokes get weaker and weaker
but far from being baffled, the audience is delirious,
jujube-jubilant. They demand an encore from the now
glad-rags and no-bones men, who freakishly comply.

Following the show Gene goes to Olive's and they
head for the sea, for Brighton. What seems like sand
on the floorboards is really spilled turtle food. A
warm, balmy midsummer night finds Olive wearing
only a black and white striped swimsuit that constantly slides down to reveal her perfect, if featureless,
breasts. The sight prompts desire in Gene, who point-
lessly adjusts his red, white-seamed trunks.

From where they're perched on Brighton Pier he
tries to kiss her but he can't—their foreheads clash.
Olive pouts in frustration. A life of lust, devoid of sex,
just isn't worth moving through, for her.

Gene is equally vacant. His depths are deserted
without a ghost to offer.

☐■ ■

Havoc pens her story, her nails marvelously manicured, her outfit another flouncy corduroy affair, this
time augmented with ludicrous felt appliques of birds
and little birdhouses. She captures Cynthia's story.
Cynthia, it turns out, is Havoc's younger sister to go-
go boot. Havoc ends her article with a poem:

> *I cut my plastic toenails*
> *Ha! I'm still alive.*
> *My hair grows too in*
> *kitchen-scourer curls*
> *attesting, all points to the contrary,*
> *that days and nights have moved*
> *their slug-tails trailing, nay, nixed*
> *over the ribs of the drying board*
> *where they imbed like mold*
> *and epic.*

Caked with enthusiasm, she's the first to return to
the former world, where she keeps working on her
column. "Can a lethargist change his spots? Can
Leopold bloom? Consider these adventures of myself,
and oh, of that comedian Gene (whatever happened
to) Plantagenet . . . "

Pola, too, she'd come to recognize as Tutti, the little
child who'd lead them.

☐■ ■

At a drive-in movie theater mysteriously adjoining one of Brighton's grandest hotels, Gene and Olive give passion one last blast. The movie details the adventures of Pinkie, a Catholic pervert, who gets along fine until he meets Bella. Olive wears a blue and white striped t-shirt and jeans with a broken zipper over her flawless body.

"Are these parking meters?" Gene questions about the speakers. He fiddles with the stubborn knob 'til it tunes into the radio station he'd always hoped for. And like that, he and Olive are back in his flat, four-postered in his bed. His ghost now flies frequently out of his restored Mephistophelean backward-tail. It thrives curdled in tea and airy in mousse. It clouds the bath water like candle wax and traces Olive's seamy lip gloss. She sighs.

Colonel has yet to show. "He was in my way, anyhow," Gene whispers to Olive, before outlining her with his tongue while planning his lust-infringed new act.

For N.,
Who Won't
Want It

*b*onnie, the strongest yet strangest girl, worked in a trophy shop. Second to wig stores, which survive solely off the things they front, trophy shops are the only outlets of their kind which exist entirely in a vacuum. Well, apart from Hoover repair shops.

From behind the thigh-high counter Bonnie stared out through the dust-streaked, cluttered window onto the dull streets of downtown Fargo. She was surrounded by glittering tokens to be twice-collected. On them plaudits are scratched like so many golden fleas.

In fact, Bonnie herself was the World's Greatest Lover, a loving B-cup buttercup, but no one knew it yet. Her hands were on her hips as locals eyed her politely while standoffishly cherishing her for her predicaments, which made their own lives interesting.

She dreamt the window was a bed-framed canvas on which was detailed the body of N., the boy who brought down her government. They'd met in Paris or London, she hadn't decided which yet, and he was an angel who'd slipped through the system. He'd ushered into her life the welcome rut of synchronicity, emphasis on sin, and enhanced her coddled world that always seemed to be accompanied by the sound of descending harp strings.

He should have left her for half the things she'd done but he stayed on, dangling like a hanged-man Christmas tree ornament.

What she loved most about him were his bare floorboards and the way the bubble-bath scent lingered in the cracks just as it did in the crevices between his perfect toes. And how he came to her seemingly straight from heaven, with no middleman — with all that this implied about divine intervention.

He appeared to her one day in the cellar of her three-story home, where she lived with her mother and her father, an elevator operator who'd obtained Bonnie's job for her, as the trophy shop bordered the building he commandeered.

The man in the cellar was called N. for reasons of anonymity known only to him, and he had eyes the color of skin that had been submerged in ice-water with surface skim as effective as a Tupperware lid. N. spoke to Bonnie in fragments and drew a self-effacing portrait. He'd materialized to her before, but she didn't know where yet. His brown hair was like flapper fringe, always in southern movement.

Theirs was an immediate intimacy and he insisted

on keeping hidden. "I'm illegally . . . insane," he offered, although Bonnie suspected he was an alien, an immigrant, from some far-flung island. European countries were distinct islands to her mind, and it was from one of these she was certain he had fled.

So at work she waited until the clock, as anticipated as a jailer's key, struck to unchain her and she could go and check on him.

Her mother, Zenia, a minx in her day and still a luxury at present, asked, "Are you going to that basement again?"

"Mom, I'm thinking about turning it into a rumpus room," Bonnie replied. "It'd be great."

Zenia returned her attention to the t.v., where she halfheartedly watched a game show called "Some Like It Not." "All the same, I'd watch out for black widows if I were you. Or bats, even."

"Oh come on, Mom! And just how are bats going to get into the basement?" Bonnie called as she descended. Her words rose above her like a cartoon caption.

"Well, I'm glad you called it a basement. It's not a cellar, you know. Not with that nice floor we put in."

Bonnie looked around for N., who was nowhere to be found. She ran back up the carpeted wooden stairs.

"Mom, have you been home all day?"

"I went to my garden club, honey, is that enough for you?"

"I'm not accusing you, Mom." Bonnie went to her room where she closed the chintz curtains. She changed clothes into jeans, a t-shirt, and a flannel shirt with the sleeves torn off.

"How nice, you've got your playclothes on now," Zenia observed as her daughter reappeared.

"That's right, Mom. I'm going out for a few minutes."

Zenia returned to the grip of the broadcasted competition.

Bonnie reasoned N. probably sought nature, because that was what he was missing from his native land. So she wandered through a wood only to be spotted by a deer who fled quickly, frightened off, no doubt, by her checked shirt.

In fact it was another kind of flora and fauna N. sought, and by more than chance Bonnie was reunited with him in the artificial shadows of the Bison Bar. In the buzzing neon light, N. looked like the bone in fine china.

"You're not a ghost, are you, 'cos I never love beneath the ground," Bonnie protested. "It's my own version of 'below the belt.' "

"And you're saying I'm beyond the pale," N. conceded quietly. "No, I can assure you, I'm not a ghost."

"I didn't think you were, but I had to clear that up." Bonnie ordered a martini, in honor of her mother. "How did you get out today?"

"The front door. As soon as Zenia went out."

"If I told her about you, she'd probably let you stay, you know. You wouldn't have to sneak around. Besides, I'd be careful if I were you, the neighbors are very observant." Bonnie caught herself. "Oh, Lord, I sound just like my mother!"

"No one was around."

Bonnie stirred her drink with the olive-swollen swizzle-stick. "I wish I knew just a little something about you."

"You know that I'm here, don't you?"

"Y-yes."

"Let that be all that matters, my Bonnie. Just as surely as you brought me into your life, just as certainly I'll stay."

Bonnie put down her stemmed glass and kissed N., her heart pulling to and fro like a bumper car. She drove him home after the city had drawn in on itself. He slipped through her bedroom window to drift down to his space in the proposed rumpus-room, stopping off in the kitchen to scrump for an apple.

Next day at work Bonnie mused over her tiny feet. "Wear thick socks!" shoe salesmen were always advising, as if it were the first she'd heard of it. She wished, too, she were a little less of a bouncing ball doting on N.'s sing-along words, happiest only when she was in the air. Her love, when it came to him, was like hallucinating without the company of a fever.

Bonnie longed to be more like her mother, who'd go out umbrella-less even in the most inclement of weathers. It was as if she thought her twisted coathanger of a halo would protect her while everyone else suffered. It was weird, especially considering that her mother was a child, albeit a toddler, of the Depression.

And I am a child of depression, Bonnie thought, exasperated. If only she could be at home, playing with her two cats, Rami and Smems, and their imaginary kittens, (sic) and (sp). She could share them with N. and she knew he would love the part about the kittens, especially because the parent cats were both males.

A customer came in, wearing a drab tweed coat, forlorn and overworn. Fingers protruded from his knitted glove, which held a mangled receipt. The lenses of his heavy-handed glasses were humid.

"I've come to collect this loving cup," he said. "It may have been here a while—we were going to award it to Buddy Holly at his concert here, but Mother Nature had other ideas."

Bonnie looked as if she were loaded with blanks.

"There might be some confusion," the man continued, "because the trophy came via a place called Neasden. That's in North London, England. What happened was a fan from there had bought the trophy at an auction but then he kind of had second thoughts and decided it belonged right here in Fargo. I've taken my time in picking it up, but I'm sure your boss knows about it even if you're not clear on it."

"I'm clear, I'm clear," Bonnie assured him. "But I need some time to look through the back room for it. Could you come back tomorrow?"

"Sure thing. What time?"

"A quarter to four?"

"Okay. By the way, I'm Jim. I'm president of the Fargo-Moorhead chapter of the Buddy Holly Fan Club. And v.p. of the Roger Maris one."

"Nice to meet you."

"And you're?"

"Bonnie."

"Okay, Bonnie. Quarter to four."

"Make it more."

"How's that?"

"No—nothing. When I was little I used to think that if things rhymed, they had to be true."

"That'll be the day," scoffed Jim. "But then who am I to say? You may just have something there."

Jim left and Bonnie stared at the air outside which resembled Jim's fogged glasses. She kept staring to stave off a panic attack: she'd taken the trophy in question home one day to show her parents, and then promptly forgotten about it. The last she could remember of it was Rami and Smems were rubbing up against it, as if to polish it with their fine fur, in the basement.

But then N. had appeared and taken precedence over everything.

Now, if she couldn't find the trophy or if her boss caught her bringing it back to the shop, she'd have to lie. And lying had to be easy, she reasoned. Start one lie and another tended to tag along. Lies, no doubt, were like stray dogs, traveling in packs.

It wasn't the first thing Bonnie had ever lifted from the shop. She'd once taken a knockoff gold record of

Hank Williams' greatest hits with her father in mind, as a Christmas present for him. But upon considering her father's feelings for the hillbilly Shakespeare, she felt it might usher Dad's new year in with melting-snow new tears, and she thought she couldn't stand that. His job, with its rapid descents and gasping, almost apologetic ascents, was earthbound enough, like wings-akimbo graveyard statuary.

When Bonnie arrived home, N. was brazenly in the front sitting room, languishing while watching a black-and-white t.v. made color by a flag of cellophane striped blue, clear, and green. "Where's Mom?" Bonnie asked, kissing his cold forehead. "And why are you watching that funny t.v.? There's a better one in the living room. Honestly, my parents' idea of culture is a religious convention, make that a Billy Graham one. I wish I could get out of this place. Could we leave, N.? Could we get out the way you came in and go back where you came from?"

She paused. "Can you talk to me just this once?"

"What do you need to know?"

"Where you came in would do, for a start. Where you lived before, what you used to do."

"I was born at home with a midwife. The house was in North London but the name of the place probably wouldn't mean much to you."

"Why were you born at home?"

"I don't know; I never asked. I don't talk to my mom, full-stop."

"How about your dad?"

"My father was a Teddy boy, do you know them?" N. sat up and smiled then, and his face lit up like a jumpsuit junk gem. "He worshipped the American 1950s, but then had his own personal kind of nostalgia."

"You were close to him?" Bonnie asked as Rami and Smems came in, in tandem, and jumped on N. to knead him, articulating for Bonnie as they often did.

"Oh, no," N. responded to Bonnie's question. "The opposite. In fact he pressured me to get a job. If it weren't for him I'd probably still be in my room playing soldiers. In the room I was born in, that is."

"You're so lucky to have that continuity," Bonnie sighed. "Although I've lived in this boring place all my life I've never had any attachment to it. I've never wanted to *stay*. I'm just the oddball dreamer who everyone knows will never escape."

"It's not that I wanted to stay, Bonnie. It's that I didn't want to be out either. But I got a job out. I got a job selling things door-to-door."

"Not the Fulham Brush Man?"

"Something like him."

"How did you stand that?"

"I didn't, very well. Then I sold shoes for a while."

Bonnie tucked her tiny feet beneath her where she sat on the settee.

"Oh, I could have fit you," he said as though fading from her grasp. "I could have fit you like a glove."

He stopped and then went on. "I returned home, broke. To avoid my father's wrath I hid inside a trophy bound for America. I didn't want to come. I didn't want to go. I don't want anything. But then I found you." He held out a golden bristle. "Take one end," he commanded Bonnie. "Tie with me a lover's knot." But the strand was like a shiny, wavering fiber optic behind Bonnie's beaded curtain of tears, drifting from her sight.

"N., what should I do?"

"Help me back downstairs," he requested. "I'm still here; it's the world that's pulling away." Bonnie held his fledgling arm and helped him to the basement, where he slipped into the loving cup.

Bonnie's parents found her in the basement surrounded by matchstick soldiers, flat, featureless trouble dolls. The flames had spread around her but avoided their protective inner circle where, too, a tiny heart remained and caused the skip on the song "Kaw-Liga" whenever Bonnie's father tried to play the straw-colored Hank Williams disc his daughter had gifted him with once when she was able.

"The most graphic thing I know of is breaking apart from the one you love," Bonnie told her very first customer the day she returned to work, trophy in tow. But the man, placing an order for the Guys and Gallows Poker Club, just winked his response. He knew her reputation and admired her.

◻◼

The
Continuity
Girl

a *nita Lose had a solid history of separation.*
Lorella adjusts her Hollywood horned-owl
glasses; she's a demon in diamante. She ignores the
spasm-like, periodic cursor on the screen and gets up
from her chrome and contac'd kitchen chair.

In the sea of film, Lorella's no minion, more a min-
now, but oh, does she aspire. Oh, does she kid. Her
apartment she calls the Spawn Ranch, so prolific and
profligate are her ideas which multiply like tadpoles,
assuming tadpoles provide and conquer. Lorella has
ultimate faith in her ideas, as if they alone generate
and perpetuate the lone lightbulb in her workspace.

The suggestive bulb remains on, even in the day—
an eternal flame. She leaves it that way because her
English boyfriend Robey had once told her how he'd
taken a lightbulb from the men's toilet in the Marquee
in order to have something to write his review by,
upon his return home.

Lorella knows many things, and one of them is that she'd never get that desperate. So she keeps a dozen lightbulbs, cushioned as eggs, on hand in the cupboard.

Lorella has a notorious, grievous lack of attention span. Forget span, even a *scan* would be a notable improvement. Her inability to concentrate is legendary; it even intrudes (Robey insists) upon her sex life. But although she could never follow a plot, she's made the movie screen her target and with an archer's grace and determination she'll strike, with her written romances.

If Cupid had a better chance of getting a treatment seen Lorella would never know it, having — on top of everything else — an ironic deficiency.

So while the overhead bulb burns efficiently and quietly, Lorella sighs. She hugs the refrigerator to stop its humming because she has another fetish: her intense fear of noise. She likes quiet words, too, like melodrama which carries with it a kind of hush-baggage, the kind porters gently relieve you of.

She glances lovingly at her vintage, de-belled telephone, at its colloquial number penciled-in whisper-like, in archaic, pneumonic tones. MOnroe 6-2454 might well have been PA 6-5000, such was her devotion to a time she was out of. The necessary answering machine winks like the cursor she's abandoned, but she knows the call it connotes is to tell her to meet her writers' group the next morning in Farmer's Market.

They always meet there, and then, but must have thought Lorella needed reminding.

Lorella wears carefree, Doris Day-gingham to the gathering and remembers, just, to remove her earplugs. The plugs, once a cloudlike godsend from a complimentary airline kit, are now almost a nuisance, mere spongy conduits sucking and absorbing each vibration's nuance like a vindictive personal stereo. As a result, Lorella now hears sounds constantly, even in previously idle objects. Everything has the voice of an irritant: washing machines, air filters, footsteps all cackle and crackle, mumble-muffling, mocking her.

"Here she is," announces Barham, self-decried ringleader of the group.

"Hi all," Lorella replies, careful not to scrape the legs of the chair against the asphalt as she pulls it away from the outdoor table.

"Don't look now," says Dean, "but a very prominent producer is at ninety degrees, over by the oranges."

"Maybe I should ask for his autograph," Priscilla intones.

"I wouldn't want it," says Lorella, "unless it was on a check."

Her group reprimands her with assorted glances, but she inwardly rebels for she is as strong as she is undermined. When the producer leaves, her friends settle into their meagre meals and the business of critiquing each other's work.

"I don't know," says Dean to Barham. "The piece just didn't have much reality for me."

Barham sits back and lights a cigarette. "Reality's just a subculture. Don't you think, Lorella?"

But Lorella is busy eying a persistent fly. Finally she looks up over her Lolita-confectionery glasses. "It's like some unattainable vice. Therefore it holds no attraction for me." She swings at the fly and knocks over a salt shaker. Superstitious, she won't look back at it, wary of her lot.

The fly, missed by a mile, now lands on the edge of Lorella's plate. She reaches into Priscilla's bag to retrieve a paperback about impressionist art, rolls it, and hits her place-setting gavel-style. The fly is now a blotch on a riverbank of misty flowers.

"Do you mind?" Priscilla scolds. "If you've got some sort of aggression toward me, why don't you just say so?"

"I'm sorry, guys," Lorella says, tearfully. "It's just that I'm thinking of leaving L.A. I might go to England for a while."

"Oh, how lovely!" purrs Priscilla.

"But what about your career?" asks Dean.

"Hey, you don't have to live here to break in," Barham lies. "Hollywood is anywhere. It's a state of mind."

"A state of mine-fields, you mean," Lorella insists. "Living in Tympany Alley and it's always trash day, always six a.m. and your headboard is right up against the alley. And the sun barges through the cheap curtains."

"Maybe you need to get away," Dean agrees.

"What are you going to do with your computer?" asks Priscilla.

Heading back to her apartment, Lorella ponders her outburst against the fly. Her actions disturb her so much she becomes a wrong-way driver on an on-ramp to the Santa Monica Freeway. She backs up, pushed and prodded by several angry car horns, each a degree off-pitch to its neighbor.

She sleeps that night in dreams of Robey, whom she met when she was dating a friend of his. That night for the first time in her life she'd wished she were out with someone else and her wish was granted in Robey, who appeared all dimples and dalyrimples, a rustic ruse/charm. Lorella questioned her then-boyfriend about him later, although she and Robey had already made an assignation.

"Him?" her boyfriend had scoffed. "He's loaded. His father owns a manure farm somewhere in Lancashire, I think."

"He can talk a lot," Lorella continued. "Maybe he thinks he can hold people in check with his dimples."

"Dimples? Are you sure that wasn't dirt?"

Lorella smiled shyly and told him she needed some time on her own. Her boyfriend was heartbroken and tried everything to find her, to win her back, but she proved as elusive as a bookmark.

On the plane to Manchester Lorella keeps her computer on her lap like a meal tray. The flight attendants give up; there's no one sitting next to her anyway. She wears rick-rack short-shorts, more hee-haw than hem.

Lorella's hayride glow stands out like a bonfire in the sterile shadows of Manchester Airport, which she scans for a phone to call Robey. She'd left Los Angeles on Halloween morning and it had been that day progressively across America: goblins and sugar-gremlins beneath her, a perfect underworld. Now, on All Saints' Day in Altrincham, Robey answers his phone.

"I'm here at the airport, here in Manchester," Lorella reports.

"You should have told me you were coming," Robey growls, but he can't disguise his chirp—he's pleased she's come and when he collects her, he looks at her tight-covered thighs which emerge from the curtain of her clothes.

"I thought I did," she says, wearily, and Robey remembers how she'd once hedged her bets, certain she could emerge from the maze at Hampton Court. He had to go in and find her seated resolutely on a stone bench, completely uninterested in coming out.

He takes her luggage and her laptop, which she won't surrender. "My scripts are in there."

"What are you working on, that 'Separation' one?"

"Yeah, among others."

"Well, you're far more fortunate than I. I'm doing a retrospective about New Romantics and trying to find one song that's still listenable. I should warn you: you might have to listen to 'Seven and the Ragged Tiger'. 'Fade to Gray.' 'Musclebound.' "

Lorella's eyes well up, deep enough for wishes.

"Nah, don't worry," he continues. "I've been listening at my office."

"I think I need some sleep."

"And sleep you shall have." Robey places her doll-like in his bed and he is her blanket, tucked between her legs.

Robey goes to his office after Lorella has slept twelve hours and shows no sign of ceasing. He dodges her suitcase which is like a ticket barrier. Her body in his bed, more laundry to do. He sighs.

Lorella awakens to the sound of hooves and when she peers out the window wearing just a sketchy slip, a troop of soldiers breaks into applause. It is a moment of sympathetic magic.

She has showered and shaved her pubis by the time Robey returns. He is dreary and disillusioned and speaks to her of Indonesia, where they might rave in the moonlight under natural phosphorescence.

"You could come," he speaks to her shorn part, and her mind slips forward and aft, never resting on the bedknob-slippery present.

Operation:
Estrangement

*t*amira's laminate identity evolved labyrinthine. It involved the postman and a colored cat named Peepers. But it championed the one who came back, oblivious to all the drama.

It was after she made a prank phone call to him that Tamira stopped loving him. His voice sounded too confident and made her certain that she could never find a window back to the unspecified Thing They Had. The mutual mystery, that one-sided mirror. Aren't they all?

So she married seeking redemption, on a ribbon-grasping rebound. She arranged the particulars with her betrothed in a wine bar in Greenwich. In an area lulled by pubs, crowded by them, even, Tamira paid too much so she could sit.

They made the deal as she doodled on a flighty cocktail napkin. She scribbled until her curlicues became delete marks.

Her fiancé was a good man, just and unreachable. The best kind. They would rent a post-boomtown flat in Docklands if they moved in together at all. There, they would live like ghosts.

After their town hall ceremony they went to Paris for their honeymoon. Tamira was as buoyed as the hovercraft, including the drops. Six hours later, they slept in a tiny room. She was wakened in the night by her husband, who slapped the mattress in his dreams and tried to scoop away a large bug that didn't exist.

Tamira paid him off in guitars and moved into the flat alone. The top half of Canary Wharf was dark of late, beckoning to be hit by low-flying aircraft. The Hobbs kettle left behind in her kitchen was cosied with internal water fur which skimmed the surface like amiable manta rays, like life rafts.

In the room she'd chosen as hers—obviously the child's room—she went to hang her market clothes in the closet. Then she started: a snake, coiled as an extension cord, was in the corner, left as an unworkable luxury.

Tamira didn't like snakes. It was nothing personal; it was just the way they moved, how it was like cursive writing.

She had to knock on several doors before she found a neighbor but once she did, the bashful man offered to remove the snake and keep it in his flat until morning, when he'd call the RSPCA. He put on his calf-length navy blue coat for the walk to Tamira's, and said little, nodding sweetly when she invited him for coffee one day soon.

Excitement over, Tamira sat in her bent-willow chair, which a mover had dropped in a place she'd never let it stay, and she wept.

Who did she miss now? Her new husband, who'd effortlessly charmed her with his brand of bare-bulb elegance? The One Who Came Before who was, objectively, so self-serving he always aced it? Her childhood pet, Linc? The snake? The man who'd removed the snake and thereby rescued her?

She slept that night in an unmade bed and had dreams linked thematically by a quirky, substantiated fear of heaven. Tamira woke the next midmorning, looking love-worn. She prepared to go into work, where she was a presenter on a television show. Her allotment was entitled "Gas Food Ligging" and was a kind of social Armageddon for beginners, best just before end. She served as a cheerleader for movers and shakers who most resembled marionettes and hand-puppets minus the blood-impetus, the motivation.

Tamira presented her pop news while wearing a pained, painted smile and then went home.

Soon she became friendly with a shared cat she named Peepers because he was fall-colored. No doubt he had as many names as flats he visited; some of them were probably the right moniker. But to Tamira he was Peepers.

Canary Wharf had a pointless laser-light show that night, the night Peepers went missing. The waves and noise were like an air raid, widespread panic. It reminded Tamira of how her father used to rage at skywriters who'd stitch the message they'd been hired to write on a seamless summer sky.

"I don't know," Tamira had replied. "To some the words might appear as a welcome mat. A 'Wipe Your Feet' for angels and other flying things."

This was when she was approaching her phobia of paradise, but didn't want to admit it. It was around the time that she knew, as she sat on smooth sand, half-looking out at unblemished water, there couldn't be another heaven, for she was in the only one she'd been promised.

Such a realization led to her indoctrination in Church Noir, and she plundered. Her rosary beads against her chest at night were heavy globes of sweat. The afterlife was a restless, accusatory place like her own small town. She bled from both, and became another tale of suburban flight. The same old run-of-the-millennium story.

In a bigger city, her first television appearance was scrapped, rendering her a snip of parenthetical celluloid. But it took another country for her to prevail, and to learn to end her segments with a sassy "And then I woke up!" as a distancing device from the stories she relayed.

There were media guardians; Tamira was a media gargoyle. And she loved it. She loved sitting in the green-with-envy room, adored the house-of-cards sets, everything.

But in her own life, like a religious convert or recovering addict, she began to backslide. Like a deejay's turntable, she began to slip.

The first casualty was her old boyfriend, whom she started to love again. It made her so permanently flushed it was like a brand of personal weather. She caught sight of him turning corners right ahead of wherever she was going, the way you see someone who's just dead.

But Tamira knew it was her hometown that was giving her the sleight and not the boy at all, and that she would have to get over it. So she stayed on as happy as possible, in love or out of it, in her new place.

When she and the postman found the cat Peepers' body sprawled beneath the collection times posted on the pillar box, they both mourned. Tamira ran through the Greenwich foot tunnel to blot her grief. At the other end, in the train station, the ticket collector sat in a window of candlelight by choice. His shadowed visage startled Tamira backward, and she returned to her flat and back to bed.

When she got up, Peepers was plainly visible from the kitchen window, padding a wall with his shrewd paws. Tamira saw Peepers, as did her neighbor, the postman, and everyone else who played with the communal feline.

But then, they never saw Peepers again. It wasn't that he was gone: he'd just changed his roaming pattern, adjusted his radius, and its rays took him someplace else, outside of even their most temporary reach.

◼ Hazy-ography

i f you parted the unruly ivy like curls off a bullying young face, you'd read on the flaking wall the slogan "David Bowie Tells the Truth."

Ann Farley has seen it and heard all the jokes about it being prehistoric cave-painting, written in primitive a long, long time ago. And about how someone should slap a preservation order on it, were anyone to care.

The wall surrounds, a lazy choker, a house once lived in by Lillie Langtry. Its carriage house is squatted by a man who sells spirituality, doles it out like church-bazaar sugared teas.

Ann doesn't mind buying but she can't stand to be given. Something in her chemistry precludes her receiving gifts graciously, and renders the final fourth of the year, which it is, a painstaking, treacherous time.

She passes by the wall but doesn't salute it or anything. Her arms are full of provisions from Brixton Market, where it's always hothouse summer. Ann goes down the chipped-incisor stairs to her basement flat and puts the groceries down on the warped, wavy linoleum. She checks her hair, a color as permanent as cut-price lipstick, and scrutinizes her makeup, which she learned to apply by copying the cover of David Bowie's *Pin-Ups*.

If you consider Bowie's then-penchant for wearing eyeshadow on his forehead, you should get some idea.

But don't necessarily take it from me. Me, for whom, in my younger days, the color blue-black was nigh-mystical. Look upon me instead as a barker-angel. And remember: even the Virgin Mary was upstaged by a bird (and that was just the beginning).

Ann's copiously-covered bedroom wall has examples of Bowie's foray into Kirlian photography. Suggestive wreaths of seeming hair look like smoke-rings blown by one *pure*.

Her flat feels as if it has pets, but it doesn't. And she walks around muttering to herself, "Don't Worry," as if it will take hold, a stick perch in a metal bird cage.

She has vital days; she has lifeless days. Does it really matter to you? Why not me, a sensitive gargoyle hunched over the edges of her soft cornices, in sharp danger of ruining her life? I could give you initials like a better part of town and a plusher, more intricately-anagrammed towel.

"As thick on the ground as blades of grass" has never seen this trampled park and the dog that rules over it. Ann had seen the dog at the news-agent's earlier, tied outside by where the flowers are bunched with rubber bands and bolt-upright in buckets. The dog took one sniff of the carnations and lifted his leg over their peculiarly pink blossoms.

And carnation was the flower she'd thrown to Bowie when he was a Diamond Dog.

(Or was that Zircon?)

Ann sits in the melting-cold park waiting for Gary, of the carriage house. He appears, wearing a snorkel-parka over his nightshirt, a sleepwalker who thinks ahead.

(There are those who'd say that I remind them of Patti Smith. But then, there are those who'd say anything.)

Gary gives her her allotment of ecstasy and throws in a bonus, special K. Back inside it's the extra that undoes her. She doesn't want anything free; she doesn't deserve it. Besides, how dare he think her affections and loyalties can be bought? Ann consumes the K in anguish, to put the present out of sight, like opened Christmas gifts stored away, cluttering space.

Behold! I stand in her black garden and knock. And play a mean game of doorbell ditch. In her dressing room I can see the shrines she's made, to Bowie, to Nick Cave, to Youth, to me. I can see her alarm clock, and it's not by her bed.

I go inside, the front door is open, and her head is in her duvet which she's dragged, felled prey, into the living room.

Over and Lover: interchangeable, aren't they?

Steeped in rock lore, I blacken teeth. Saint Benzedrine. I'd be wary to see what I'd create in the night, in dark sleep.

Now Ann's not doing anything but flopping around like a death-bird, a moth. "My hair," she fusses. "It only looks the way I want it to when I'm staying in."

Now, really, is this the kind of sentiment you need? Is this what words are for?

She's buried in air, worried why some dope in North London wouldn't kiss her, overburdened with symbolism.

Next morning, she clears her flat. Her possessions are acidic home-soil to a vagabond. She moves toward a commune, Glastonbury, via the carriage house by the shrubbery wall.

If I need to find her, I will. Then, like the cold, I'll draw ranks around her.

About the Author

Susan Compo is the author of a previous collection of short fiction, *Life After Death and Other Stories*. Raised in Orange County, California, she now lives in London, where she is a freelance writer.